ALSO BY ROBERT CHARLES WILSON

A HIDDEN PLACE

MEMORY WIRE

GYPSIES

THE DIVIDE

A FOUNDATION BOOK   DOUBLEDAY

NEW YORK LONDON TORONTO SYDNEY AUCKLAND

THE
DIVIDE

Robert
Charles
Wilson

S

A FOUNDATION BOOK
PUBLISHED BY DOUBLEDAY
a division of Bantam Doubleday Dell Publishing Group, Inc.
666 Fifth Avenue, New York, New York 10103

FOUNDATION, DOUBLEDAY, and the portrayal of the letter F
are trademarks of Doubleday, a division of
Bantam Doubleday Dell Publishing Group, Inc.

Library of Congress Cataloging-in-Publication Data
Wilson, Robert Charles, 1953–
    The divide / Robert Charles Wilson. — 1st ed.
        p.   cm.
    "A Foundation book."
    I. Title.
    PR9199.3.W4987D58   1990
    813'.54—dc20

89-33211
CIP

ISBN 0-385-24947-0
ISBN 0-385-26655-3 (pbk.)

Printed in the United States of America

January 1990

FIRST EDITION
DC

D. 2
19.95

PART I
PRIVATE EXPERIMENTS

I

Such an ordinary house. Such an ordinary beginning.

But I *want* it to be an ordinary house, Susan Christopher thought. An ordinary house with an ordinary man in it. Not this monster—to whom I must deliver a message.

It was a yellow brick boardinghouse in the St. Jamestown area of Toronto, a neighborhood of low-rent high-rises and immigrant housing. Susan was from suburban Los Angeles—lately from the University of Chicago—and she felt misplaced here. She stood for a moment in the chill, sunny silence of the afternoon, double-checking the address Dr. Kyriakides had written on a slip of pink memo paper. This number, yes, this street.

She fought a momentary urge to run away.

Then up the walk through a scatter of October leaves, pausing a moment in the cold foyer . . . the inner door stood open . . . finally down a corridor to the door marked with a chipped gilt number 2.

She knocked twice, aware of her small knuckles against the

ancient veneer of the door. Across the hall, a wizened East Indian man peered out from behind his chain-lock. Susan looked up at the ceiling, where a swastika had been spray-painted onto the cloudy stucco. She was about to knock again when the door opened under her hand.

But it was a woman who answered . . . a young woman in a white blouse, denim skirt, torn khaki jacket. Her feet were bare on the cracked linoleum. The woman's expression was sullen—her lips in a ready, belligerent pout—and Susan dropped her eyes from the narrow face to the jacket, where there was a small constellation of buttons and badges: BON JOVI, JIM MORRISON, LED ZEPPELIN. . . .

"You want something?"

Susan guessed this was a French-Canadian accent, nasal and impatient. She forced herself to meet the woman's eyes. Woman or girl? Older than she had first seemed: maybe around my age, Susan thought; but it was hard to be sure, with the make-up and all.

She cleared her throat. "I'm looking for John Shaw."

"Oh . . . *him.*"

"Is he here?"

"No." The girl ran a hand through her hair. Long nails. Short hair.

"But he lives here?"

"Uh—sometimes. Are you a friend of his?"

Susan shook her head. "Not exactly . . . are you?"

Now there was the barest hint of a smile. "Not exactly." The girl extended her hand. "I'm Amelie."

The hand was small and cool. Susan introduced herself; Amelie said, "He's not here . . . but you can maybe find him at the 24-Hour on Wellesley. You know, the doughnut shop?"

Susan nodded. She would look for "Wellesley" on her map.

Amelie said, "Is it important? You look kind of, ah, worried."

"It's pretty important," Susan said, thinking: Life or death. Dr. Kyriakides had told her that.

———

Susan saw him for the first time, her first real look at him, through the plate-glass window of the doughnut shop.

She allowed herself this moment, seeing him without being seen. She recognized him from the pictures Dr. Kyriakides had shown her. But Susan imagined that she might have guessed who he was, just from looking at him—that she would have known, at least, that he was not entirely normal.

To begin with, he was alone.

He sat at a small table in the long room, three steps down from the sidewalk. His face was angled up at the October sunlight, relishing it. There was a chessboard in front of him—the board built into the lacquered surface of the table and the pieces arranged in ready ranks.

She had dreamed about this, about meeting him, dreams that occasionally bordered on nightmares. In the dreams John Shaw was barely human, his head unnaturally enlarged, his eyes needle-sharp and unblinking. The real John Shaw was nothing like that, of course, in his photographs or here, in the flesh; his monstrosities, she thought, were buried—but she mustn't think of him that way. He was in trouble and he needed her help.

Hello, John Shaw, she thought.

His hair was cut close, a burr cut, but that was fashionable now; he was meticulously clean-shaven. Regular features, frown lines, maps of character emerging from the geography of his fairly young face. Here is a man, Susan thought, who worries a lot. A gust of wind lifted her hair; she reached up to smooth it back and he must have glimpsed the motion. His head turned—a swift owlish flick of the eyes—and for that moment he did *not* seem human; the swivel of his head was too calculated, the focus of his eyes too fine. His eyes, suddenly, were like the eyes in her dreams.

John Shaw regarded her through the window and she felt spotlit, or, worse, *pinned*—a butterfly in a specimen case.

Both of them were motionless in this tableau until, finally, John Shaw raised a hand and beckoned her inside.

Well, Susan Christopher thought, there's no turning back now, is there?

Breathing hard, she moved down the three cracked steps and through the door of the shop. There was no one inside but John Shaw and the middle-aged woman refilling the coffee machine. Susan approached him and then stood mute beside the table: she couldn't find the words to begin.

He said, "You might as well sit down."

His voice was controlled, unafraid, neutral in accent. Susan took the chair opposite him. They were separated, now, by the ranks of the chessboard.

He said, "Do you play?"

"Oh . . . I didn't come here to play chess."

"No. Max sent you."

Her eyes widened at this Holmes-like deduction. John said, "Well, obviously you were looking for me. And I've taken some pains to be unlooked-for. I could imagine the American government wanting a word with me. But you don't look like you work for the government. It wasn't a long shot—I'm assuming I'm correct?"

"Yes," Susan stammered. "Dr. Kyriakides . . . yes."

"I thought he might do this. Sometime."

"It's more important than you think." But how to *say* this? "He wants you to know—"

John hushed her. "Humor me," he said. "Give me a game."

She looked at the board. In high school, she had belonged to the chess club. She had even played in a couple of local tournaments—not too badly. But—

"You'll win," she said.

"You know that about me?"

"Dr. Kyriakides said—"

"Your move," John said.

She advanced the white king's pawn two squares, reflexively.

"No talk," John instructed her. "As a favor." He responded with his own king's pawn. "I appreciate it."

She played out the opening—a Ruy Lopez—but was soon in a kind of free fall; he did something unexpected with his queen's knight and her pawn ranks began to unravel. His queen stood in place, a vast but nonspecific threat; he gave up a bishop to expose her king, and the queen at last came swooping out to give checkmate. They had not even castled.

Of course, the winning was inevitable. She knew—Dr. Kyriakides had told her—that John Shaw had played tournament chess for a time; that he had never lost a game; that he had dropped out of competition before his record and rating began to attract attention. She wondered how the board must look to him. Simple, she imagined. A graph of possibilities; a kindergarten problem.

He thanked her and began to set up the pieces again, his large hands moving slowly, meticulously. She said, "You spend a lot of time here?"

"Yes."

"Playing chess?"

"Sometimes. Most of the regulars have given up on me."

"But you still do it."

"When I get the chance."

"But surely . . . I mean, don't you always win?"

He looked at her. He smiled, but the smile was cryptic . . . she couldn't tell whether he was amused or disappointed.

"One hopes," John Shaw said.

———

She walked back with him to the rooming house, attentive now, her fears beginning to abate, but still reluctant: how could she tell him? But she must.

She used this time to observe him. What Dr. Kyriakides had

told her was true: John wore his strangeness like a badge. There was no pinning down exactly what it was that made him different. His walk was a little ungainly; he was too tall; his eyes moved restlessly when he spoke. But none of that added up to anything significant. The real difference, she thought, was more subtle. Pheremones, or something on that level. She imagined that if he sat next to you on a bus you would notice him immediately—turn, look, maybe move to another seat. No reason, just this uneasiness. Something *odd* here.

It was almost dark, an early October dusk. The streetlights blinked on, casting complex shadows through the brittle trees. Coming up the porch stairs to the boardinghouse, Susan saw him hesitate, stiffen a moment, lock one hand in a fierce embrace of the banister. My God, she thought, it's some kind of seizure—he's sick—but it abated as quickly as it had come. He straightened himself up and put his key in the door.

Susan said, "Will Amelie be here?"

"Amelie works a night shift at a restaurant on Yonge Street. She's out by six most evenings."

"You live with her?"

"No. I don't live with her."

The apartment seemed even more debased, in this light, than Susan had guessed from her earlier glimpse. It consisted of one main room abutting a closet-sized bedroom—she could make out the jumbled bedclothes through the door—and an even tinier kitchen. The place smelled greasy: Amelie's dinner, Susan guessed, leftovers still congealing in the pan. Salvation Army furniture and a sad, dim floral wallpaper. Why would he live here? Why not a mansion—a palace? He could have had that. But he was sick, too . . . maybe that had something to do with it.

She said, "I know what you are."

He nodded mildly, as if to say, *Yes, all right.* He shifted a stack of magazines to make room for himself on the sofa. "You're one of Max's students?"

"I was," she corrected. "Molecular biology. I took a sabbatical."

"Money?"

"Money mostly. My father died after a long illness. It was expensive. There was the possibility of loans and so forth, but I didn't feel—I just didn't enjoy the work anymore. Dr. Kyriakides offered me a job until I was ready to face my thesis again. At first I was just collating notes, you know, doing some library research for a book he's working on. Then—"

"Then he told you about me."

"Yes."

"He must trust you."

"I suppose so."

"I'm sure of it. And he sent you here?"

"Finally, yes. He wasn't sure you'd be willing to talk directly to him. But it's very important."

"Not just *auld lang syne?*"

"He wants to see you."

"For medical reasons?"

"Yes."

"Am I ill, then?"

"Yes."

He smiled again. The smile was devastating—superior, knowing, but at the same time obviously forced, an act of bravery. He said, "Well, I thought so."

———

Susan had no relish for this talk of illness. Her father's illness had dominated her life for almost a year, keeping her on a dizzying rollercoaster of falling grades, missed deadlines, serial flights to California. In her graduate work she had been doing lab chores for Dr. Kyriakides, a study involving the enzyme mechanics of cancerous cell division; and it had been too painful an irony, that shuttle between the colonies of laboratory cells and her father's bed, where he was dying of liver cancer. There is such a thing, Susan thought, as too much knowledge. She could not bear this meticulous understanding of the mechanism of her father's death. She began to dream of malignant cells, chromosomes writhing inside their nuclei like angry, poisonous insects.

She suspected that the work Dr. Kyriakides gave her was a kind of charity. He had explained to her—the sophisticated European to the parvenu Californian WASP—that this was good and useful, that a person in mourning ought to have tasks to attend to. She was skeptical but grateful, and within a month she began to admit he was right: there was solace in the library stacks, in the numbers that marched so eloquently across the cool amber screen of her PC terminal. Her grasp of the work began to deepen. Dr. Kyriakides was a brilliant man; the book would be brilliant. Their relationship was not a friendship but something that, in Susan's opinion, was much finer. She began to feel like a colleague. She took her own work more seriously.

Then, in August, Dr. Kyriakides had escorted her to a Greek restaurant in the mezzanine of a downtown hotel and had ordered impressively for both of them: medallions of lamb, an expensive wine. She had wondered with vast apprehension whether he meant to proposition her.

Instead he leaned forward and gazed into the bowl of his wine goblet. "A quarter of a century ago," he said, "when I was just out of Harvard, and the government was paying so many smart people to commit such stupid acts, I did something I should not have done."

It was the first time she'd heard the name John Shaw.

———

You can see his illness, she thought now. Waves of discomfort seemed to sweep across John's face. He clenched his teeth a moment; then he said, "I'm sorry."

"Dr. Kyriakides wants to see you," Susan said. "The changes you're going through aren't necessarily irreversible."

"He told you that?"

"He can help."

"No," John said.

"He told me you might react this way. But there's no one else you can go to. And he *wants* to help."

"I think it's beyond that."

"How can you be sure?"

"No offense intended. But my guess is as good as Max's."

"But," Susan began, and then faltered. The pain he was suffering—if it was in fact a physical pain—overtook him again. The smile that had grown small and ironic now disappeared altogether. His knuckles whitened against the arm of the chair; his face seemed to change, as if a great variety of emotions had overtaken him, a sudden shifting . . . she thought of wind across a wheatfield.

She was frightened now.

She said, "What can I do? Can I help?"

He shook his head. "You can leave."

The rejection was absolute. It hurt.

Susan said, "Well, maybe you're right—maybe he *can't* help."

It was her own moment of cruelty. But it caught his attention. She persisted, "But what if you're wrong? There's at least a chance. Dr. Kyriakides said—"

"Fuck Dr. Kyriakides."

Susan was quietly shocked. She stood up, blushing.

"No, wait," John said. "Leave your number."

"What?"

"Leave your number. Or your address, your hotel room. Write it down. There's paper over there. I'll call. I promise. We can talk it over. But right now—I need to be alone right now."

She nodded, scribbled down her name and the hotel, moved to the door. She turned back with the idea of making some final entreaty, but it was pointless. He had dismissed her; she was as good as invisible. He sat with his eyes closed and his head pressed

between his hands . . . containing himself, as if he might ex-
plode, Susan thought as she hurried down the walk into the cold
October night; or shutting out the world, as if it might rush in
and drown him.

2

Amelie Desjardins understood very quickly that she was having
a bad day—and that it would only get worse.

George, the manager at the Goodtime Grill, had put her on a
split shift for the week. She worked from eleven-thirty to two-
thirty, took an afternoon break, then she was back from five-thirty
to eight o'clock at night. Which pretty much fucks up your day,
Amelie thought, since she was too tired to do much after the
lunch rush except trek back to St. Jamestown for a nap—her nap
having been interrupted this afternoon by the woman looking for
John.

Which was mysterious in itself, and Amelie might have worried
more about it . . . but she had other things on her mind.

First she had come in to work a little late, and George climbed
down her throat about it. Then there was prep and set-up, and it
seemed as if every salt shaker in the place had gone empty all at
once, which was a hassle. Then Alberto, the cook, chose this
terrific time to start coming on to her, and *that* was a balancing

act you wouldn't wish on a trapeze artist, because you *have* to be on good terms with the cook. A friendly cook will juggle substitutions, fill your orders fast, do you a hundred little favors that add up to tips . . . but when you came right down to it Amelie thought Alberto was about as oily as the deep-fat fryer, which, not coincidentally, he seldom cleaned. Alberto rolled through the steamy kitchen like a huge, sweating demiurge, when he wasn't peeking through the door of the changing room trying to catch a waitress in her underwear. So it was "You look really good tonight, Alberto," and winking at him, and sharing some of her tips, and then getting the hell out of his way before he could deliver one of his patented demeaning gropes. It amounted to a nasty kind of ballet, and today Amelie was just slow enough that she was forced to dislodge Alberto with her elbow—which left him in a vengeful sulk throughout the dinner rush.

Amelie was philosophical about working at the Goodtime. It was not a prestigious restaurant, but it was not a dive, either; it was a working-class wine-and-beer establishment that had been in business for thirty-five years in this location and would probably be edged out before long by the rising rents—judging by the plague of croissant houses and sushi bars that had descended on the neighborhood. At the Goodtime, there was always a fish-and-chips lunch special. Fifteen tables and a few framed photographs of the Parthenon. The walls had recently been stuccoed.

Amelie had been working at the Goodtime for almost a year now and she had a kind of seniority, for what it was worth—the newer girls would come to her with questions. But seniority counted for shit. Seniority did not prevent the occurrence of truly rotten days.

Like today, when the new girl Tracy innocently grabbed off a couple of her regulars and seated them in her own section. Like today, when she was stiffed for a tip on a big meal. Like today, when some low-life picked a busy moment to walk out on his check—which George would sometimes forgive, but, of course, not *today;* today he docked her for the bill.

It was maybe not the *worst* day Amelie had ever experienced. That honor was held by the memorable occasion on which a female customer had come in during the afternoon, ordered the Soup of the Day, meticulously garnished the soup with crushed soda crackers, then retired to the Ladies and opened her wrists. Both wrists, thoroughly and fatally. Amelie had found her there.

George told her later that this had happened four times during the history of the Goodtime and that restaurant toilets were a popular place for suicides—strange as that seemed. Well, Amelie thought, maybe a suicide doesn't *want* a cheerful place to die. Still, she could not imagine taking her final breath in one of those grim salmon-colored stalls.

So this was a bad day, but not the *worst* day—she was consoling herself with that thought—when Tracy tapped her shoulder and said there was a call for her on the pay phone.

Bad news in itself. No one was supposed to take calls on the pay phone. She could think of only one person who would call her here.

"Thanks," she said, and delivered an order to Alberto, then checked to see if George was hanging around before she picked up the receiver.

It was Roch.

Her intuition had been correct:

A *very* bad day.

He said, "You're still working at that pit?"

"Listen," Amelie said, "this is not a good time for me."

"I haven't called you for months."

"You shouldn't call me at work."

"Then come by my place—when you get off tonight."

"We don't have anything to talk about."

Amelie realized that her hand was cramping around the receiver, that both hands were sweaty, that her voice sounded high and throttled in her own ears.

Roch said, "Don't be so shitty to your brother," and she recognized the tone of offhanded belligerence that was always a kind of warning signal, a red flag. She heard herself become placating:

"It's just—it's like I said—a bad time. I can't talk now. Call me at home, Roch, okay?"

"You'll be home tonight?"

"Well—" She didn't like the way he pounced on that. "I'm not sure—"

"What, you have plans?"

She took a deep breath. "I'm living with someone."

"What? You're doing *what?*" The outrage and the hurt in his voice made her feel a hot rush of guilt. Crazy, of course. Why should she consult *him?* But she hadn't. And he was family.

But she could never have told him about Benjamin. She had been hoping—in a wistful, unconscious way—that the two of them would never have to meet.

The party at Table Four was signaling for her. This was, Amelie recognized, a truly shitty day.

She forced herself to say that she was living with a guy and that it might not be all right for Roch to come over, she just couldn't say, maybe he ought to phone up first. There was a very long silence and then Roch's voice became very sweet, very ingratiating: "All right, look—I just want you to be happy, okay?"

"I'm serious," Amelie insisted.

"So am I. I'd like to meet this guy."

"I don't know if that's a good idea."

"Hey! I'll be nice. What is it, you don't trust me?"

"I just—well, *call* me, all right? Call me before you do anything."

"Whatever you want."

She waited until the line went dead, then stood with her forehead pressed against the cool glass of the enclosure. Took a breath, smoothed a wrinkle out of her uniform, forced herself to turn back toward the tables.

George was standing there—hands on his hips, a monumental frown. "You know you're not supposed to use this phone."

She managed, "I'm sorry."

"By the way, the corner table? The party that was waiting for the bill? They had to leave." Now George smiled. "Tracy took your tip."

———

She was out of the place by nine.

Nine o'clock on a Friday in October and Yonge Street was crowded with the usual . . . well, Amelie thought of them as *types*. Street kids with leather jackets and weird haircuts. Blue-haired old ladies in miniskirts. Lots of the kind of lonely people you see scurrying past on nights like this, with no discernible destination but in a wild hurry to get there: heads down, shoulders up, mean and shy at the same time. It made her glad to have a home to head for, even if it was only a shitty apartment in St. Jamestown. Shitty but not, of course, cheap—nothing in this town was cheap.

She peered into the shop windows, trying to distract herself, but it was a chilly night and she felt intimidated by the warm glow of interiors and the orange light spilling out of bus windows as she trudged past the transit station. Nights like this had always seemed comfortless to her. You could smell winter gathering like an army just over the horizon. Nights like this, her thoughts ran in odd directions.

She thought about Roch, although she didn't want to.

She thought about Benjamin.

Impossible to imagine the two of them together. They were so different . . . although (and here was the only similarity) each of them seemed to Amelie endlessly mysterious.

Roch should not have been a mystery. Roch, after all, was her brother. They shared family . . . if you could call it family, an absentee father and a mother who was arrested for shoplifting with such startling regularity that she had been banned from Eaton's, Simpson's, and Ogilvy's. Sometimes Amelie felt as if she had been raised by a Social Welfare caseworker. She'd been fostered out twice. But the thing was, you learned to adapt.

Roch, her little brother, never did. They grew up in a rough part of Montreal and went to the kind of Catholic school where the nuns carried wooden rulers with metal edges embedded in them—in certain hands, a deadly weapon. The nuns were big on geometry and devotions. Amelie, however, had had her own agenda. In an era when the Parti Québecois was dismantling English from the official culture, Amelie had resolved to teach herself the language. Not just the debased English everybody knew; not just the English you needed to follow a few American TV shows. *Real* English. She had conceived of a destiny outside Montreal. She saw herself living in English Canada, maybe eventually the States. Doing something glamorous—she wasn't sure what. Maybe it would involve show business. Maybe she would manage a famous rock band.

Maybe she would wait tables.

Roch was different. He never had any ambitions that Amelie could figure out. When he was real little he would follow her around as singlemindedly as a duckling; she would tow him down St. Catherine's Street on sunny summer days, buy Cokes and hot dogs and spend the afternoon watching the Types from the steps of Christ Church Cathedral.

Roch had needed the company. He never had friends. He took a long time learning to talk and he wasn't reading with any facility until he was in fifth grade. Roch, it turned out, was slow. Not stupid—Amelie made this important distinction—just slow. When Roch learned something, he hung on to it fiercely. But he took his time. And in that school, in that place, taking your time was a bad thing. It made you *look* stupid. Not clever-stupid or sullen-stupid or anything dignified; it made you look dog-dumb, especially if you were also small and ugly and fat. Amelie had been bruised a few times defending Roch in the schoolyard. And that was when she bothered to stand up for him. A thirteen-year-old girl sometimes doesn't want to know when her idiot brother is catching flack. She thought of him that way, too—her idiot brother—at least sometimes.

But Roch *wasn't* stupid, Amelie knew, and he learned a lot.

He learned not to trust anybody. He learned that you could do what you wanted, if you were big enough and strong enough.

And he learned to get mad. He had a real talent for getting mad. Pointlessly, agonizingly mad; skin-tearing mad; going home and vomiting mad.

And then, eventually, he learned something else: he learned that if you grow up a little bit, and put on some muscle, then you can inspire fear in *other people*—and oh, what an intoxicating discovery that must have been.

Amelie trudged along Wellesley into St. Jamestown, past the hookers on the corner of Parliament, thinking October-night thoughts. She stopped at a convenience store to pick up a couple of TV dinners, the three-hundred-calorie kind. She was skinny— she knew it, in an offhand way—but her reflection in the shop windows always looked fat. Mama had been fat, with a kind of listless alcoholic fatness Amelie dreaded. Amelie was young and skinny and she meant to stay that way.

She put Roch out of her mind and thought about Benjamin instead, and that lightened her mood. She even managed a smile, standing at the check-out counter. Because Benjamin was the great discovery of her life.

A recent discovery.

He had come into the Goodtime just about six months ago, on one of those ugly spring days when the wind is raw and wet and just about anybody is liable to wander in off the street. She took him at first for one of those wanderers: a tall, benign-looking, shy man with a puppydog smile, his collar turned up and a black woolen cap plastered to his head. An oddball, but not a Type, exactly; he looked straight at her in a way Amelie appreciated. She remembered thinking the odds were mixed on somebody like that: he might tip generously or not at all . . . you could never tell.

But he did tip, and he came back the next day, and the day after that. Pretty soon he was one of her regulars. He came in late one Wednesday and she told him, "I'm going off-shift—you're late," and he said, "Well, I'll walk you home," in that straight-ahead way, and Amelie said that would be all right—she didn't even have to think about it—and pretty soon they were seeing each other. Pretty soon after that he moved out of his basement room on Bathurst and into the St. Jamestown apartment.

Benjamin was decent, well-meaning, kind.

Roch enjoyed crushing people like that.

Amelie's smile faded.

And of course there was the other problem, which she tried not to think about, because, even among these other mysteries, it was *too* mysterious, *too* strange.

The thing about Benjamin was, he wasn't always Benjamin.

————

The apartment was a mess, but it felt warm and cozy when Amelie let herself in. She kicked off her shoes, ran some hot water for the dishes, plugged a Doors tape into the stereo.

She was not deeply into Sixties rock, but there was something about Morrison: he just never sounded old-fashioned. The tape was *Strange Days;* the song that came up was "People Are Strange." Loping drumbeat and Ray Manzarek moaning away on keyboard. That real sparse guitar sound. And Morrison's voice doing his usual psycho-sexy thing.

Timeless. But she turned it down a little when she peeked into the bedroom and saw Benjamin asleep under the covers. He slept odd hours; that was one of the strange things about him. But she doubted the tape would wake him—he slept like a slab of granite.

Back to the dishes, Amelie thought.

Awright, yeah! said Morrison.

And if Roch came by—

But maybe he wouldn't. She consoled herself with that thought, bearing down with the scrub brush on one of the Chinese dragon bowls she'd bought in Chinatown. The basic fact about Roch was his unpredictability. He might say he was going to do something, but that didn't mean shit. You never could tell.

She took some marginal comfort in these thoughts, losing herself in the rhythm of the music and the soapy smell of the hot water.

She was draining the sink when the last song, "The Music's Over," faded out. She heard the click of the tape as it switched off, the faint metallic transistor hiss from the speakers . . . and the knock at the door.

————

"You should have called."

"I tried earlier. You weren't home." Roch stood blinking in the hallway. "You're supposed to invite me in."

Amelie stood aside as he came through the door.

"Place is a mess," he observed.

"I just got home, all right?"

He shrugged and sat down.

It was six months since Amelie had seen her brother, but it was obvious he hadn't let up on his gym work. He was six foot one, a head taller than Amelie, and his shoulders bulked out under his bomber jacket. All the body work, however, had done nothing for his looks. His face was wide and pasty, his lips were broad. He stood with his hands in his jacket pockets and Amelie could see them moving there, knitting and unraveling, making fists, the fingernails digging into the palms. She told him to sit down.

He pushed aside a pile of newspapers and sprawled on the sofa.

Amelie made coffee and talked to him from the kitchen. There had been a letter from Montreal: Mama was adjusting to the new apartment even though it was smaller than the old one. Uncle

Baptiste had been in town, looking for work when the Seaway trade picked up again. She kept her voice down, because it was possible even now that Benjamin might sleep through the whole thing . . . that Roch would say what he had to say and then leave. She pinned her hopes on that.

She poured a cup of coffee for him and one for herself and carried them into the living room. She sat opposite him in the easy chair, took a sip—bitter black coffee—and listened to the sudden silence of the room, the absence of her own voice.

Roch said, "I lost my job."

She put her cup down. "Oh, shit."

He waved his hand. "It was a stupid job."

Roch had been working as a parcel clerk at the BPX depot, the last Amelie had heard. This was, frankly, not a great surprise; Roch had never been good at keeping jobs. But it was not good news, either.

She said, "You found anything else?"

"I have some leads."

"What happened?"

He shrugged.

"You have any money?"

He said, "Is that an offer?"

"I don't have a hell of a lot to spare."

Roch was silent for a while. His expression was reptilian, Amelie thought, the combination of his pout and the slow, periodic blinking of his eyes. She was tempted to stare. Instead, she looked at her coffee cup.

Roch said, "You could earn some."

"What—George is gonna raise my salary because I have an unemployed brother?"

It was the wrong thing to say. Her brother paused in his blinking. *"Calyx!* Amelie, do you think I'm stupid?"

When Roch got angry he slipped into his father's vernacular: it was *calyx* this and *tabernacle* that, *maudit ciboire de Christ* and so on. Venerable backcountry curses. She shrank down in her chair. "That's not what I meant."

Roch smiled. The steady semaphoring of his eyelids began again. "Waitressing is not the only way to make money."

"I don't understand."

"I have a problem here. I have to pay rent, you know."

"Look, what do you want? Some cash? A loan?" She reached for her purse. "I can give you twenty."

"Fuck that," Roch said. "Twenty dollars? Christ!"

She waited.

He said, "Remember when we came to this city?"

Now Amelie was silent for a beat.

"Yes," she said.

"You remember what we did then?"

Deep breath.

"Yes."

"Maybe the time has come again."

"No," Amelie said.

"What?"

"I said *no!* All right? Is that clear? I won't do it."

"I don't like the tone of your voice."

"I don't care." She couldn't look at him.

He said, "You don't care that I'm broke—that I'll be out on the street?"

"No. I meant—"

"Hey, I'm your little brother! You look after me!"

"So you want to *pimp* for me? Is that your idea of a good career move?"

Christ de calyx! As her father might have said.

But Roch only smiled. "You can keep your day job."

"Well, *fuck you!*"

Her reaction was involuntary. She hated him for bringing up the subject. Sure, she had done some things in the past. She was barely seventeen when they left home; Roch was younger. They slept on warehouse roofs some nights, and other nights they rented rooms in the wino hotels on Queen Street. You can't survive on the street without doing something you don't like. And so maybe she had done that—what he talked about—when they needed the money, and maybe once or twice just because they *wanted* the money . . . but that was the old days. He was crazy, coming here with a proposition like that.

So she stood up and said *fuck you* and it was a mistake, because Roch did not take well to that kind of abuse—as he had told her many times—and now *he* was standing up, inches away from her, so close she could smell the hot-metal reek of his breath. He did not blink at all. He took her wrist in a fierce grip. All that weight-lifting had made him strong.

He said, "You do it if I tell you to do it." Then he slapped her.

The slap was painful and Amelie stumbled away from him. She caught her foot against the table supporting the stereo; she fell down hard on the floor and the tape player came tumbling down after her. *Strange Days* popped out of the cassette compartment with a streamer of tape reeling after it. Amelie closed her eyes.

Opened them, and saw Benjamin come out of the bedroom.

She looked up from the floor, blinking.

Benjamin stood in the doorway with his Levis half unbuttoned and his belt undone. He was naked from the waist up. His hair was tousled. He gave Amelie a long look and then stared at Roch. He said, "Who the hell are you?"

"Never mind," Amelie said, "it's nothing." But the damage was already done.

Roch broke out into a big anticipatory grin.

"I'm her brother," Roch said. "Who the fuck are *you?*"

Benjamin stepped forward. He was as tall as Roch but less bulky —he looked emaciated by comparison. And fragile, his hairless chest exposed. He said, "I guess you were leaving."

Amelie had never heard him talk like that before.

Roch said, "Guess again."

Benjamin didn't flinch. He was looking at Roch with an expression Amelie had never seen on him before, a kind of automatic and terrible contempt . . . which unnerved Roch, who balled his fist.

"Get out of my face," Roch said.

"Get out of my home," Benjamin said.

Roch drew back his fist . . .

But Benjamin hit him in the face.

Roch just stood there, blinking, as if he was working it out in his head: *what* happened?—*what?*—then raised his hand to his nose. It was bleeding; Roch examined the blood for a long moment. Then he drew back his fist and threw it at Benjamin in a terrible, pistoning boxer's punch . . . but Benjamin moved out of the way somehow; and then Roch—who was a member of a Cabbagetown boxing club, a heavyweight—threw a couple of very serious street punches. But Benjamin just leaned around them somehow and threw a few punches of his own, little nettling jabs that infuriated the bigger man. It was crazy, Amelie thought, it was not even a fight, there was nothing fair about it; it was a humiliation. Roch was turning a bright brick red. He screamed, "Stand still, you fucking faggot!"

And Benjamin stood still, but Roch didn't respond—couldn't, maybe.

The expression on Benjamin's face was terrifying. It was a cold, radiant confidence in his own supremacy, an unblinking ferocity. He moved closer to Roch now, stood so that he was separated from him by a few inches of air. Amelie imagined the space between them as white-hot, flashing with some kind of invisible lightning. She could not see all of Benjamin's face now but she could see Roch's, and she was stunned by the fear he began suddenly to radiate. Staring into Benjamin's eyes and seeing . . . what?

Something awful.

Benjamin said one word, very low; Amelie thought it was, "Leave."

Roch turned away like a whipped child and lurched to the door.

Before he left he turned and pointed a trembling finger down at Amelie. He looked as if he was about to burst into tears.

"You," he said. "You . . . *cunt*. . . ."

And then fled.

And Amelie turned to look at Benjamin, and understood all at once what had happened:

He *wasn't* Benjamin right now.

He was John.

———

He looked down at her in that way she hated, a mixture of pity and condescension at the back of his eyes. He started to say something—it might have been "I'm sorry."

"Get out," Amelie said. She was embarrassed, hurt, humiliated —she couldn't stand him looking at her. "Just leave."

His eyes lingered a moment longer. Then he nodded.

He went back to the bedroom for a shirt and a jacket, and then he left . . . but he stopped on the way out and picked up something that had slipped off the lampstand during his fight with Roch. It looked like a scrap of paper, Amelie thought . . . with maybe a phone number written on it.

3

It was near midnight when John called.

Susan had eaten dinner at the hotel coffee shop and had come back to her room to read, hiding from this strange city in the pages of a book. She had a Joyce Carol Oates novel and a Travis McGee mystery, both from the paperback rack in the lobby. She loved to read, and after her father's death she had thought about giving up the sciences and starting over as an English major. She decided against it for a couple of reasons. Her taste in reading was way too catholic—she read Faulkner and Stephen King with approximately equal relish. And she was afraid of destroying the pleasure she took in these books. Susan was not analytical about fiction; she had been twelve years old before she understood that books had *writers,* that they had to be manufactured, somehow, like shoes. Better not to inquire too closely into cherished illusions. . . . They were fragile.

Tonight the Joyce Carol Oates seemed a little too architectural; she slipped into the welcoming embrace of Travis McGee. Old

Travis had mellowed a lot in his later books. He had more second thoughts these days. She liked that.

With the drapes open she curled up in bed, propped up with pillows behind her and a view of the city lights running north to the horizon. She was three chapters into the book and inclining toward sleep when the phone rang.

She picked it up expecting Dr. Kyriakides, but it was late for him to be calling; she couldn't place the voice at first.

"John Shaw," he said.

Well—obviously. But he sounded younger on the phone. You couldn't see his eyes; his eyes were ancient.

Susan struggled to assemble her thoughts. "I'm glad you called—"

"I think you're right," he said. "I think we should talk."

"I agree. Uh, maybe we can get together tomorrow?"

"You're at the Carlton?"

"Yes."

"I'll meet you in the lobby. Is noon all right?"

"Of course—sure—"

"See you there."

And then the line went dead, and she was left sleepy and amazed, staring at the receiver in her hand.

———

She rode the elevator down at five minutes to noon the next morning and found him waiting.

He was standing by a marble pillar, dressed in worn Levis, track shoes, and a blue windbreaker over a T-shirt, with his hands tucked into his jacket pockets. Susan moved toward him with her heart beating hard, as his head swiveled owlishly and his eyes focused in on her.

"I'm sorry," she said. "I don't think I did a very good job yesterday. I didn't know how to start."

"You're in a tough position," John said. "The messenger with bad news."

"Plus—I guess I was a little frightened."

He smiled. "Of me?"

She laughed, but it was true. She *had* been frightened. Still was. But it was easier now, at least a little. "Where do we go for lunch?"

"Depends. I don't have a lot of cash. Are you on an expense account?"

"It's paid for."

"By Max?"

"Ultimately."

"Well, there's a decent Japanese restaurant around the block. I'm sure Max can afford it."

"Sounds fine," Susan said.

She had never eaten Japanese food but didn't want to admit it. The atmosphere in the restaurant was traditional: koto music and waitresses in tight kimonos. She felt somewhat gauche, lost among the rice paper screens; she let John order for her.

The waitress brought miso soup in a wooden bowl. No spoons —apparently you were supposed to pick up the bowl like a cup. John said, "You're not used to this."

She forced a smile. "Redondo Beach WASP. We never ate anything more challenging than Mexican. I remember a lot of TV dinners."

"The main course is tempura. Nothing scary. Unless you have a problem with shrimp?"

"No, that's fine. You know, I learned to eat Cantonese and Szechuan in college. Just never got around to Japanese."

John turned his attention to the soup. He ate meticulously, Susan observed; almost mechanically. When the bowl was empty he pushed it aside and ignored it. "Max knows I'm ill."

Straight to the point, Susan thought. "He suspected it."

"Is he still working with prenatal growth regulators?"

"Not officially."

"But on his own?"

"Some animal research."

"Out of curiosity, I wonder, or guilt?"

Susan frowned. "I'm sorry?"

He waved his hand—never mind.

The waitress brought sashimi on wooden plates. "Thank you," Susan said. The waitress bowed and returned a "Thank you."

"It might be easier," John said, "if you just told me what you know about me. We can begin there."

But it was a tall order: *What kind of monster do you think I am?* Susan told him what Dr. Kyriakides had explained to her—that John was the product of a clandestine research project conducted in the fifties. Before his birth he had received an intrauterine cocktail of cortical growth regulators, human hormones Dr. Kyriakides had isolated under a classified government grant. The purpose of the research was to produce a superior human being, specifically in the neocortical functions—the most highly evolved functions, such as intelligence.

John's smile was fixed. " 'Highly evolved'—sounds like Max. He told you all this?"

"At greater length. And with more breastbeating."

"He *does* feel guilty."

"I have the impression he always did."

"Did he mention that his 'government grant' was by way of a client operation of the CIA? That his name came up twice in the Church Committee hearings?"

"Yes. He says they were funding everything in those days— LSD at McGill, exotic botany at Harvard. Postwar insanity."

"Did he also mention that he was the closest thing to a father I had for the first several years of my life?"

"Something like that."

"And that he farmed me out for adoption when the project was closed down?"

"He didn't have a choice."

"But now he wants to talk . . . because he thinks I'm dying."

"I should never have said that! I'm sorry—I just wanted to get your attention."

"But it's possible?"

"The animal studies have been mixed," Susan admitted.

"Some animals have died."

She looked at the table. "Yes."

The tempura arrived then. Susan picked at hers. It was good, but she'd lost her appetite.

John ate vigorously.

———

When the check arrived Susan used her credit card and filed away the customer copy. John said, "Are you up to walking a little?"

She nodded.

"It's a good day for it. Autumn is the best time of year in this city." He stood up and pulled his windbreaker over his T-shirt. "I don't get many afternoons like this."

They rode the College streetcar west to Augusta. The day was cool but endlessly sunny, the sky a shade of blue you never saw in L.A. When the streetcar stopped, John climbed down through the rattling mid-car doors and offered her his hand. How dry his skin is, Susan thought . . . and then scolded herself for thinking it. He wasn't an animal, after all.

He led her south through a maze of ethnic markets, fish stalls, vegetable bins, used-clothing outlets. This was Kensington Market, John said, and it was his favorite part of the city.

It was also crowded and more than a little bewildering—no two signs in the same language—but Susan felt some of the carnival atmosphere, maybe picking it up from John. He took her to a café, a sidewalk table under an umbrella and far enough from the fish stalls that the air was tolerable. He ordered two cups of fierce cappucino. "Legal drugs." Smiled at her. She sipped the coffee. He said, "Well, maybe I am dying."

Her cup rattled against the saucer. "Do you always have these two-track conversations?"

"You mean, is this a manifestation of my superhuman intellect? Or just an annoying habit?"

"No, I don't mean that. I mean—well, if you don't want to talk about it—"

"Max must have warned you, surely? John the monster." He startled her by closing his eyes. "You're wearing Levis and a brown sweater with a checked collar showing at the neck. You have brown hair, blue eyes, a mole under your right cheekbone and another one just under your ear. You have both hands on the table; the nail is chipped on your left index finger. You don't wear nail polish. The building behind you is catching the sunlight; it has twenty-eight rectangular windows facing the street and a revolving door with a mango cart parked on the sidewalk in front of it. The cart vendor is wearing a yellow plaid shirt and a black beret. A grey Nissan Stanza just drove past, southbound—it should be at the intersection by now." He opened his eyes and stared at her. "You come from Southern California and you're timid with people. You have an exaggerated respect for Dr. Kyriakides—take my word for it—and some unresolved feelings about your own father. You have a suppressed speech impediment that begins to surface when you talk about your home, which you don't like to do. You think you like me, but you're still a little frightened. You—"

"Stop it!"

There was a silence. Susan blushed deeply.

John said, more gently, "I don't want you to forget what I am."

"As if I c-could!" She thought about leaving. She wasn't sure her legs would hold her. "How can you know all that about me?"

"Because you're a book. Not just you, Susan. Everyone. A book of gestures and twitches and blinks and grimaces."

"Do you *want* me to be frightened of you?"

"Only . . . appropriately frightened." He added, "I'm sorry."

Gradually, she relaxed back into her chair. "Do you still want to talk?"

"Do you still want me to?"

She took a deep breath. "Yes."

"To you, or to Max?"

"Talk to me if you want. But only Dr. Kyriakides can help you."

"If in fact he can."

"If." She didn't want to risk lying—assuming it was possible to lie to him.

"It's a game of chance, then, isn't it? Roulette."

"I'm not the doctor."

"You're the doctoral candidate."

"It's not exactly my field. I never worked directly with Dr. Kyriakides on this, except for a few tissue studies."

He shook his head. "I'm not ready to talk to Max."

"Then me. Talk to me."

He gave her another long, speculative look. Susan could not help wincing. My God, she thought, those eyes! Not the windows of the soul . . . more like knives. Like scalpels.

"Maybe it would be good to talk," he said. "It's been a long time since I talked to anyone."

"I'm not going anywhere," Susan said.

She asked whether he had been having symptoms.

"Episodes of fever, sometimes dangerously high. Transient muscular weakness and some pain. Fugue states—if you want to call them that."

"Is that what was happening yesterday?"

He nodded.

"I don't know what you mean by a 'fugue state.' "

He sipped his cappucino. "May I tell you a story?"

The formal research project had ended when John was five years old. He was adopted by a childless couple, the Woodwards, a middle-income family living in a bleak Chicago suburb. The

Woodwards renamed him Benjamin, though he continued to think of himself as John. From the beginning, his adoptive parents were disturbed by his uniqueness. He didn't do especially well in school—he was contemptuous of his teachers and sometimes a discipline problem—but he read beyond his years and he made conversation like an adult; which, the Woodwards told him, was very disrespectful.

"Jim Woodward was a lathe operator at an aerospace plant and he resented my intelligence. Obviously, a child doesn't know this, or doesn't want to admit it. I labored for almost eight years under the impression that I was doing something terribly wrong—that he hated me for some fundamental, legitimate reason. And so I worked hard to please him. To impress him. For example, I learned to play the flute. I borrowed a school instrument and some books; I taught myself. He loved Vivaldi: he had this old Heathkit stereo he had cobbled together out of a kit and he would play Vivaldi for hours—it was the only time I ever saw anything like rapture on his face. And so I taught myself the Concerto in G, the passages for flute. And when I had it down, I played it for him. Not just the notes. I went beyond that. I *interpreted* it. He sat there listening, and at first I thought he was in shock—he had that dumbfounded expression. I mistook it for pleasure. I played harder. And he just sat there until I was finished. I thought I'd done it, you see, that I'd communicated with him, that he would approve of me now. And then I put the flute back in the case and looked at him. And he blinked a couple of times, and then he said, 'I bet you think you're pretty fucking good, don't you?' "

"That's terrible," Susan said.

"But I wasn't convinced. I told myself it just wasn't good enough, that's all. So I thought, well, what else is there that matters to him?

"He had a woodworking shop in the basement. We were that kind of family, the Formica counters in the kitchen, Sunday at the Presbyterian church every once in a while, the neighbors coming over to play bridge, the woodwork shop downstairs. But he had quality tools, Dremel and Black and Decker and so on, and he took a tremendous amount of pride in the work he did. He built a guitar once, some cousin paid him a hundred dollars for it, and he must have put in three times that in raw materials, and when it was finished it was a work of art, bookmatched hardwood, polished and veneered—it took him months. When I saw it, I wanted it. But it had been bought and paid for, and he had to send it away. I wanted him to make another one, but he was already involved in some other project, and that was when I saw my opportunity—I said, 'I'll build it.'

"I was nearly thirteen years old. I had never so much as touched his woodworking tools. 'Show me,' I said. He said, 'You'll never manage it. It's not a beginner's project.' I said, 'Let me try.' And I think now he saw it as *his* big opportunity . . . maybe this would teach me a lesson. So he agreed. He showed me how to work the tools and he gave me some books on luthiery. He even took me to lumberyards, helped me pick out decent woods."

John paused to sip his cappucino. "I worked on the guitar that summer whenever he was out of the house. Because it was an experiment—you understand? This would be the communication, he would see this and love me for doing it, and if he didn't—all bets were off. So I took it very seriously. I cut and sanded, I routed the neck, I installed the fretwire and the tuning machinery. I was possessed by that guitar. There was not a weekday afternoon through July or August I was out of the house. I was dizzy with lacquer fumes half the time. And when he came home I would hide the project . . . I didn't want him to see it until it was ready. I cleaned the tools and the workshop every day; I was meticulous. I think he forgot about it. Thought I'd given up. Until I showed it to him."

Susan said, "Oh, no."

"It was perfect, of course. Max probably told you what his research had suggested, long before it was fashionable science—

that the neocortical functions aren't just 'intelligence.' It's also dexterity, timing, the attention span, the sense of pitch, eye-hand coordination—things as pertinent to music or luthiery as they are to, say, mathematics. Jim Woodward thought he'd found a task that was beyond me. In fact, he could hardly have picked one I was better suited to. Maybe that guitar wasn't flawless, but it was close. It was a work of art."

Susan said, "He hated it."

John smiled his humorless, raw smile. "He took it personally. I showed him the guitar. The last varnish was barely dry. I strummed a G chord. I handed it to him . . . the final evidence that I was worthy of him. To him it must have been, I don't know, a slap in the face, a gesture of contempt. He took the guitar, checked it out. He sighted down the neck. He inspected the frets. Then he broke it over his knee."

Susan looked at her hands.

John said, "I don't want sympathy. You asked about symptoms. This is relevant. For years I had thought of myself as 'John' while the Woodwards were calling me 'Benjamin.' After that day . . . for them, I *was* Benjamin. I became what they wanted. Normal, adequate, pliant, and wholly unimpressive. You understand, it was an act. They noticed it, this change, but they never questioned it. They didn't want to. They welcomed it. I worked my body the way a puppeteer works a marionette. I *made up* Benjamin. He was my invention. In a way, he was as meticulous a piece of work as that guitar. I made him out of people I knew, out of what the Woodwards seemed to want. He was their natural child—maybe the child they deserved. I played Benjamin for almost three years, one thousand and eighty-five days. And when I turned sixteen I took my birth certificate and a hundred-dollar bill James Woodward kept in his sock drawer, and I left. Didn't look back, didn't leave a forwarding address . . . and I dropped Benjamin like a stone." He took a sip of cappucino. "At least I thought I did."

"What are you saying—that *Benjamin* was a symptom?"

"He *is* a symptom. He came back."

The cool air made Susan shiver. She watched three teenagers in leather jackets and spike haircuts stroll past, eyes obscure behind Roy Orbison sunglasses.

John said, "I noticed other problems first. Minor but disturbing. Auditory hallucinations, brief fugue states—"

"When was this?"

"Three years ago, more or less. I was living in a cabin on a gulf island off the coast of British Columbia. I blamed a lot of it on that—on the isolation. But then, without any kind of warning, I lost two calendar days. Went to bed on Sunday, woke up Wednesday morning. Well, that was frightening. But I was methodical about it. I tried to reconstruct the time I'd lost, pick up on any clues I'd left. I found a receipt in a shirt pocket, nine dollars and fifty-five cents for groceries at a supply store in town, a place I never shopped. It was a family grocery not much bigger than my cabin, and when I went in to ask some questions the woman back of the check-out desk nodded at me and said, 'Hello, Benjamin! Back again?' "

"And the fugues persisted?"

"I'm lucky to have a day like this . . . a day to myself."

Susan didn't know what to say.

He drained his cappucino and turned the cup over. "You want to know what it feels like? It's like learning to do a puppet act . . . and then forgetting which one of you is which. The boundaries fold away. Suddenly you're inside the mirror looking out."

"I see."

He regarded her steadily. "Is that what you expected—you and Max?"

"Not exactly."

He stood up. He said, "I think I'm dying because I can't remember how to be John Shaw anymore."

———

He walked her back to the hotel.

He was quieter now, almost reticent, as if he had said more than he meant to. He walked with big, impatient strides and Susan had to struggle to keep up. She was panting for breath by the time they reached the lobby.

He turned to face her at the door, wrapped in his jacket, almost lost in it. What had he said? *The boundaries fold away. . . .* He said, "You've done your job. You can go home with a clear conscience."

"That wasn't the idea. We hoped—Dr. Kyriakides thought—if you came to Chicago—"

"Why? So he can watch me fade away?"

"He has some ideas that might help."

"He has a pathological curiosity and a bad conscience."

"You haven't spoken to him for twenty years."

"I don't want to speak to him."

"Well, *what*, then? You stay here? You curl up in that cheap apartment until you disappear?"

She was startled by her own words—John seemed to be, too. He said, "I'm glad we talked. I'm glad you listened. You want to help. That's nice. And you have. But I'm not ready to leave here."

"You don't have to make that decision now. I'll be in town for a week." She could extend her reservation at the hotel. Surely Dr. Kyriakides would pay for it? "We can talk again."

John looked closely at her and this time, Susan thought, it was very bad, that X-ray vision stare, the sense of being scanned. But she stood up to it. She stared back without blinking.

He said, "I . . . it might not be possible."

"Because of Benjamin?"

He nodded.

"But if it *is* possible?"

"Then," he said quietly, "I know where you are."

He turned and stalked away into the cool air.

She watched him go. Her heart was beating hard.

Because, she realized, it *matters* now.

She had come here determined to do a job . . . to intercede for Dr. Kyriakides, to find John Shaw and say her piece and get it over with.

But that had changed.

Now she wanted something else.

She wanted him to live.

4

John Shaw left Susan at the hotel and began the walk back to St. Jamestown. He understood that he was losing himself in this bright, cool autumn dusk—that he was fading with the light.

He'd been fortunate this time. He had been lucid for more than a day and a half. That was uncommon and—if what the girl said was true—it would be increasingly rare.

He could feel the good time ending now. The sky was a luminous, inky blue; the trees in the park looked etched in charcoal. This was always the first sign of the change: this sudden, heightened vividness of things. For most of his life he had lived in a universe of symbols, language and memory, nouns and verbs; strange to have the world itself, its crude essence, suddenly crowding into his mind. Strange to look at an arc of cloud across the cold sky and lose awareness of it as a meteorological event, to lose all the taxonomy of clouds—the word "cloud" itself—it all being washed away by naked vision, as if some vital boundary had been erased; as if he had somehow *become* the cloud.

He stood immobilized on the sidewalk with his head canted up until the feeling passed. Then he frowned and walked on, hands burrowing deep into his pockets.

Fading, he felt more alive than ever.

Cling to it, he thought. It was a clear, cold evening and he didn't want to give it up. For a time he was tempted to turn back to the hotel, knock on Susan Christopher's door and say to her, *Yes, if you can cure me, if Max can cure me, I'll do what you want . . . I've lost too much of my life already.*

But he didn't turn back. That direction was the past: Kyriakides, the Woodwards, the gulf island. Too much to embrace. In any case, he doubted that Max had any real answers. Susan had admitted as much. Max was the perennial scientist, still anxious—but not admitting it, perhaps not even to himself—to see his most important experiment through to a conclusion.

The thought evoked a vivid memory of Max as he must have looked to a five-year-old: stubbled, huge, wise, and aloof. Glints of light off his wire-rimmed glasses, which he would sometimes allow John to wear. The lenses turning Kyriakides into a looming, distorted monster. Angles of light through crystal: the laws of diffraction.

But the daylight was failing now. The streetlights winked on. Almost home, John told himself, if you could call it that, the two dingy rooms Benjamin shared with Amelie. It was Benjamin who made the serious decisions now, such as where to live and with whom. He was Benjamin most of the time, and it was like a dream, these long days of absence, not an utter loss of consciousness but a cloudy capitulation: floating underwater down some dark, twisting conduit. Occasionally he would blink at the world through Benjamin's eyes, wake up and think, *I, I, I.* And then sink back into the darkness, one more lost thing.

He did feel some sympathy for Amelie, even though she regarded him as an illness of Benjamin's—and that was strange, too, to be considered a disease. He remembered frightening away the man who had attacked her the night before. Her shame and her anger. But maybe she was right; maybe he had made things worse.

But he couldn't worry about that now. He hurried up the steps and through the door, down the gray stucco hallway into the apartment, closing himself in. Amelie was off at work. John locked the door and turned on the TV. The babble of voices rose up like a physical presence and he gazed without comprehension at the screen: rioting on the West Bank, the arc and explosion of tear-gas canisters.

Thinking: Hold on.

But it was like falling asleep. You couldn't resist forever. Couldn't stay awake forever.

Faltering, he thought about Susan.

He had liked talking to her. She knew what he was, and that stripped away the burden of pretense. There was the inevitable chasm between them, the biochemical and physiological gap— what Max had once called an evolutionary gulf. But that was inevitable, and she was at least aware of it . . . and acknowledging the gulf seemed somehow to narrow it.

The talk had been good. But the talk had also evoked old, unpleasant memories; memories that were difficult to suppress at the best of times. And these were not the best of times.

He knew what to do about Susan Christopher. Tell her firmly that he wasn't interested. Hope that Max wouldn't press the matter.

Fade, if fading was inevitable.

That was what John Shaw meant to do.

But it occurred to him, closing his eyes, that Benjamin might have other plans.

He groped after the thought and lost it. Too late now. The space behind his eyelids seemed to fill with a bright and unforgiving light. His head throbbed and ached. The change was coming, too fast and fiercely to resist. Memories surfaced like phosphorescent sea-creatures: Susan's face, their conversation, Kyriakides and the Woodwards, the shimmering veneer on the face of a hand-made guitar . . . all these pieces of himself, fragile as a china cup for one weightless moment . . . and then gone, shattered, dispersed.

He slept. And someone else awoke.

5

"He's refusing treatment?"

Dr. Kyriakides sounded angry, his voice growling through the phone lines from Illinois.

Susan said, "At the moment—yes."

"He's not aware of the problem?"

"He's very aware of it." She repeated the list of symptoms John had recited, the recurrence of "Benjamin."

"That's not what I would have predicted," Dr. Kyriakides said. "But it might be a positive sign."

"You think so? How could it be?"

"He's capable of tremendous things, Susan—both his conscious and his unconscious mind. He's resurrected Benjamin for a reason, even if he's not aware of it. It's a response to the disease, I suspect . . . as if one suit of clothes has begun to wear out, and he's preparing to put on a second."

"But it's not the same," Susan said. "It's not *him.*"

"But in some sense it *must* be him. Benjamin is his creation. It's not something new—it can't be. Only an aspect of himself."

"But it isn't John Shaw. The John Shaw part of him is dying."

There was a pause. "Possibly," Dr. Kyriakides admitted. "In one way or another."

"Then we have to help him."

"I agree! But if he's refusing treatment—"

"He could change his mind. He said he might call back. I want to stay—at least another week. I need to talk to him again."

There was another crackling silence through the long exchange from Chicago. "I don't remember you being this enthusiastic."

"I suppose . . . it never seemed real before."

"Then you must have felt it, too."

"I'm sorry?"

"His specialness. There's something unique about John. I mean, beyond the obvious. There always has been."

"Yes," she said. "I know what you mean."

"Take whatever time you need."

"Thank you."

"Do you want a suggestion?"

"Anything."

"Talk to the other one. Talk to Benjamin."

"I'll try," Susan said.

But she had thought of that already.

———

The problem was how to begin.

She wasn't much good with people. Susan had figured that out a long time ago. She was a book-reader and she had always been good with words, but that facility did not extend to her tongue. For most of her adolescence she had been a stutterer. She loved words but could not gracefully pronounce them; people often laughed when she tried. She had retreated into muteness and spoke only when it was unavoidable. Her mother took her for sessions with a "teen counselor," who linked Susan's stuttering with her parents' divorce: a traumatic event for a twelve-year-old, yes, she guessed so. Privately, she connected the stutter with her father's grim refusal to discuss anything connected with the event, though he picked her up every weekend in his car and drove her places: the beach, park picnics, Disneyland, his apartment. Day trips, rituals of silence. *How are things at school, Susie? Fuh-fuh-fine.* Then his cancer erupted, a fierce Round One: in this corner, Laryngeal Nodes; in that corner, the Surgeon's Knife. He recovered, or seemed to, except for his voice. His conversation dimmed to a whisper. The doctors said there were devices he could use, but he refused. To Susan he seemed to have achieved a whole new identity, more gaunt and wholly withdrawn. After the surgery, she was afraid to talk to him. Afraid that her own voice might strike him as a rebuke or a taunt: *See, I still have my tuh-tongue.*

She felt infected by his silence and determined to overcome her own. She performed speech exercises. She joined the yearbook staff at high school and studied back issues of *Seventeen* for clues to the social graces. It was a scientific project—as solemn as that. She was not John Shaw, inventing a new self; but the inspiration was similar . . . a willful disguise. And it was effective; it worked; but she remained painfully conscious of the creaking machinery behind the proscenium. People would look at her oddly and she would think *Oh! I made a mistake.*

Approaching John Shaw had been hard enough, even under the cloak of impartiality. Approaching Benjamin would be even harder. Because she wasn't just a messenger from Dr. Kyriakides anymore. This had become, in a way, her own project now. And she needed her own words.

———

She began by renting a car. She chose a late-model Volvo and spent a day with her city map, learning the downtown. Then back to the hotel to shower, followed by cheap Chinese food on Spadina Avenue and another evening with Travis McGee. No one called; no one left a message.

She set her wristwatch alarm for 5 A.M. and slept with it under her pillow.

By the time it annoyed her awake there was morning light coming through the big plate-glass window. Not sunlight, but only a grey, tepid half-light and a few flakes of snow. She stood under the hot water of the shower until her skin hurt, then dressed in Levis, a cotton shirt, and a jacket. She rode the elevator down to the parking level, coaxed the Volvo to life, and drove into St. Jamestown.

She parked in front of the rooming house where John Shaw lived.

The snow evolved into a cold, steady drizzle as Susan shivered in the car. She watched the people who emerged from the rooming house, made ghostly by the condensation on the Volvo's windows. None of them was John Shaw—or Benjamin. Seven o'clock slid past. At seven-thirty she was beginning to feel not merely misguided but embarrassed—playing espionage games before breakfast. She pulled her jacket closer around her and decided she would go for coffee and a croissant—she had seen a place on Yonge Street—at, say, eight o'clock. If nothing had happened.

Moments before her deadline, Benjamin left the rooming house.

She almost missed him. Dr. Kyriakides had warned her about the possibility that Benjamin might not look much like John Shaw. Obviously his features were the same, but there were subtler clues of posture and style and movement, and from this distance—through the rain—he might have been another person altogether. He walked differently. He *held himself* differently. He stepped into the October morning, his face disguised by the hood of a yellow raincoat, and this was not John's long, impatient stride but something more diffident, careful, reserved. He paused at the sidewalk and looked both ways. His glance slid over the little Volvo without hesitation, but Susan pressed herself back into the seat.

He turned and walked westward through the rain.

Susan waited until he reached the corner; then she turned the key in the ignition and eased the Volvo into traffic.

He walked to work, which made it easier. By negotiating slowly through a couple of troublesome intersections she was able to follow him all the way to University Avenue, where he vanished into the lobby of a tall, anonymous Government of Ontario building.

She continued up the street, parked, bought herself breakfast at a fast-food restaurant. A sign on the wall announced a thirty-minute limit, but Susan found the table attendant, a Jamaican woman, and said she had an appointment at eleven-thirty—was it okay if she sat here out of the rain? The woman smiled and said, "We don't get a big rush till noon. Make yourself comfortable, dear."

She finished the Travis McGee while nursing a cup of coffee. A steady rain washed over the tinted atrium-style windows. The air was steamy and warm.

At ten she ran across the street for a copy of *Time* magazine, came back for a second coffee and left the lid on.

At eleven-thirty she left the restaurant and walked a block and a half to the building where Benjamin worked.

She stationed herself in the lobby as the lunch crowd began to flow past. No sign of Benjamin. She wondered if there was a second exit. But she hadn't seen one.

At twelve-ten she asked the guard by the elevator whether there was a cafeteria in the building.

"Third floor," he said.

"Do I need a badge?"

He smiled. "No, ma'am. I don't believe it's considered a privilege to eat there."

She took a deep breath and punched the *Up* button.

———

"You're not yourself today, Benjamin," the secretary at Unemployment Insurance said; but Benjamin sailed on past, deaf to the obvious, pushing his mail cart. It was true, he was *not* himself; he was full of disquieting thoughts, thoughts he could barely contain.

He had missed a lot of work recently—more evidence that things were not as they should be. Today he had noticed his supervisor Mr. Gill eyeing him from the office behind the mail desk . . . maybe wondering whether to launch a complaint or to say something to Benjamin first; in the Provincial Government, with its labyrinths of employee protection, the process of firing someone could be tortuous. The absences were unusual, though, because Benjamin genuinely liked his job. He liked sorting the mail and pushing the cart twice a day; when the work ended he liked coming home to Amelie, at least when she had the evening off. He had fallen into the routines of his life like a sleepwalker caught up in an especially happy, luminous dream, and he would have been content to dream on forever. But something had begun to interfere with the dream—a waking-up; or perhaps a deeper, dreamless sleep.

Trouble, Benjamin thought. Trouble all around him, trouble *inside* him. He felt its pulse beat at his temples with every step. Trouble trouble trouble.

All the office clocks were creeping toward noon. He had nearly finished his run, half of the building on Bay Street, room to room and up the elevators, dropping off mail with the pretty, brightly dressed secretaries who smiled and thanked him from behind their reception desks, their barricades of computer terminals and hanging plants—their perfume mingling with the smell of broadloom and Xerography to create what Benjamin thought of as the Government Office Smell. Shouldering past the men in suits who nodded or ignored him, he was rendered invisible by his open collar: the Invisible Man. He wheeled down the corridor from Unemployment Insurance to Social Welfare with the unanswered statement now echoing in his head (I'm *not* myself—I'm *not*—

I'm *not* myself) in time with the squeak of the left rear wheel of the cart (must oil that). It was not the sort of idea he was accustomed to having. It was troubling and strange, and he knew (but did not want to acknowledge) its obvious source.

John.

The name arose unbidden, a sort of greyness. The name *John Shaw* was associated in Benjamin's mind with things hard, drab, and unyielding. Asphalt, concrete, slate. John was a dim memory, a ghost impulse, as ephemeral as the sense of *déjà vu.* But he was also a real presence, suddenly more real than he had been for years, a *demanding* presence . . . dangerous. Not just because I might lose my job, Benjamin thought, but because I might lose, might lose . . . no, but oh well, admit it, might lose *Amelie.*

Might lose that touch, voice, smile, night presence, that *(yes, say it)* love, which had entered into his life so suddenly . . . those eyes, which regarded him and in some sense created him: confirmed his suspicion that he existed. If Amelie can love Benjamin then Benjamin is real. He understood this about himself. He possessed only a few scraps of a past, some of them illusory. But the present was real. This moment, this now. And especially his moments with Amelie. What he felt for her was uncreated, was whole, was beyond suspicion.

He didn't want to lose her.

He would not allow her to be taken away. . . .

But how to stop it?

Things were happening. Things beyond his control.

Trouble, he thought, as he parked the mail cart behind the sorting desk in the basement. He rode the elevator up to the employee cafeteria, bought himself a ham-on-a-kaiser and a carton of milk; then stood petrified with the tray in his hand, staring at the woman across the room, familiar but unfamiliar, who was staring at him—and the only thought in his head was *trouble trouble trouble.*

Trembling, he carried his tray to her table. She gestured for him to sit down.

They regarded each other for a long moment, Benjamin arriving at the understanding that *she* was frightened, too; though he couldn't guess why. She was a small, nervous woman with short dark hair and brittle eyeglasses and a can of Diet Pepsi in front of her. "I'm Susan," she said.

"Do I know you?"

"I'm a friend of John's."

Benjamin doubted it. Sometimes, scraps of memory would cross the barrier between Benjamin and John—more often now than ever before. That was how he had recognized the woman in the first place. But the recognition did not signal "friend"; instead it evoked a more complex reaction, fear and hunger and hope and an old, vast disappointment almost too big to contain.

"I only have an hour for lunch," he said.

She sipped her Pepsi. "You work here?"

"In the mail room. I sort and deliver."

"Interesting work?"

"I like it." He unwrapped his sandwich but left it alone. He wasn't hungry anymore. "This is about John," he said. "Something's happening to John."

————

John my real father, he thought, John who invented me, John who created me. No, not quite that; but there was no obvious word for what John had done or Benjamin had become; no word that Benjamin knew.

He knew about John. It was a shadow knowledge, ghostly, and for a long time Benjamin had tried to ignore it. But the knowledge wouldn't go away. Useless to pretend, for instance, that he had had a childhood. For a long time he had remembered growing up with the Woodwards, but most of that was false memory, no more substantial than the picture on a TV screen. His "real" childhood was John's childhood, a confusion of threatening im-

ages (a woman named Marga, a man named Kyriakides); in fact
his childhood was no childhood at all, because "Benjamin" had
never been a child. Benjamin was born a teenager and only gradually acquired a substantial existence, imitation deepening into reflex—*the mask growing roots into the skull*, he thought, startled:
because it was a John thought more than a Benjamin thought.
Maybe John was coming back again.

So soon. Too soon.

"I was sent here by Dr. Kyriakides," Susan said, and the name
sent a shockwave up his spine. "Dr. Kyriakides thinks John might
be sick. Might be dying."

This was not the kind of information he could assimilate all at
once. His stomach was churning. He looked at his watch. "I have
to go back to work."

"I can wait," Susan said. "I have my car—I can drive you
home."

Trouble! But there was no avoiding it now.

He stood. "I get off at four."

"I'll meet you in the lobby," Susan Christopher said.

————

Rain all day, grey down the big office windows as he wheeled his
cart around; rain when he followed Susan Christopher out to her
car, red-blinking rain all up and down the dark rush-hour streets.
Benjamin sank into the front passenger seat as Susan pulled out
into the traffic. She said, "Do you know about John, about what
he is?"

"A little," Benjamin said. "I know more about him than I used
to. His brain, right? His brain is different." My brain, too, he
thought: it's where we live. Briefly, he imagined the kind of house
called a "semi-detached," two separate homes butted up against a
common wall. Noisy neighbors, Benjamin thought. Used to be the
wall was thicker; nothing came through. Now, when John was in
control, Benjamin retained some sense of his own existence, as if
he had retreated to an upstairs room where he could watch from

the window, or just float and dream, while his raucous neighbor shouted and raved.

"His brain is unique," Susan was saying. "He was made that way. There were hormones—drugs—that changed the way he grew."

"Dr. Kyriakides."

Susan nodded.

"And now that's changing," Benjamin guessed.

She gave him a second look, maybe surprised that he had guessed. She nodded. "The tissue in the brain is more fragile than anyone expected. It deteriorates—it may be doing that already."

"A mental breakdown," Benjamin said.

"Maybe. Maybe even worse than that. Not just for John—for you."

But he could not dispel the image of his brain (John's brain) as a house, a cavernous mansion, strange and multichambered—now grown brittle, dry, drafty, and susceptible to flash fires. "You don't really know what might happen."

"No, not really."

But *something* was happening; Benjamin knew it; and he guessed she was right, you couldn't burn down half a house and leave the other half intact—what happened to John would surely happen to Benjamin, too. For years Benjamin had been John's shadow, his half-self, a marionette. But in the last few months he had emerged into a real existence—a life; and when he said the word "I" it meant something; he had moved in with Amelie, who looked at him and saw Benjamin. "Benjamin," she would say. Maybe he had let himself believe that this would go on forever . . . that John would fade; that John would become the shadow, reduced at last to "John," a memory. *But now maybe we both lose. Maybe we're both memory.*

Susan drove into the core of St. Jamestown, where the peeling apartment towers stood like sentinels. She pulled up at the curb opposite the rooming house, but neither of them moved to get out. Susan turned the heater up.

Benjamin looked thoughtfully at her. "What do you want me to do?"

"I want you to help."

"Help how?"

"I want you to see Dr. Kyriakides. I want you to let him treat you."

"Can he change what's happening?"

"We're not sure. We'd like to find out."

But the idea was disturbing. He felt a spasm of unease that was clearly John's: as if John had rolled over inside him. "John doesn't want me to do that."

"He's reluctant," Susan admitted. "I've spoken to him."

Benjamin gazed at the rain. "I don't control him."

"You control yourself."

"I'm not sure—I don't know if I could do something he didn't really want. I mean, it's never come to that."

"I just want you to think about it," Susan Christopher said. "That's enough for now."

"Oh, I'll think about it." Benjamin unlatched the door. "You can count on that."

————

He crossed the rainy street to the boardinghouse, where the front door opened and Amelie stepped out, hugging herself, glancing a little nervously from Benjamin to the rental car and back. Benjamin was suddenly in love with the look of her under the wet porch awning in her tight jeans and a raggedy sweater and her breath steaming into the cold, wet air. *Not for John,* he thought: what Susan Christopher had asked for, his "help," he might give, even if it meant an end to everything he had assembled here, his real life (which might be ending anyway); but not for John or even for himself. *For her,* he thought, for Amelie on the porch in her old clothes, Amelie who had drawn him out of the vacuum of himself with a word and a touch . . . because there was a chance, at least, that he might survive where John did not, and he owed her that chance; owed her the possibility of a happy ending; or—if that failed—if everything failed—at least the evidence of his courage.

———————

Susan watched from the Volvo as Benjamin entered the rooming house.

Scary, she thought, how easy it was to accept him as Benjamin. "Multiple personality"—she had seen the movies, the PBS documentaries. But those people had always seemed just slightly untrustworthy, as if the whole thing might be—on some level—a sort of confidence trick, the nervous system's way of committing a sin without taking the blame.

This was different. Benjamin was not the product of a normal mind pushed beyond its limits. He was an invention—a work of art, a wholly synthetic creation. A "normal" mind, Susan thought, can't do that. It was a feat unique to John Shaw, as unpredictable and utterly new as the fiercely coiled cortical matter under his skull.

Unnerving.

A new disease, Susan thought. She put the car in gear and pulled away from the curb. A new disease for a new species. Hypertrophy of the mind. A cancer of the imagination.

6

Bad night for Amelie.

The rain didn't let up. Worse, she felt as if a similar cold cloudiness had invaded the apartment. Benjamin was quiet all through dinner, which was spaghetti and bottled sauce with some extra garlic and hamburger; the kind of meal Amelie assumed a man would like, *substantial,* with the steam from the cookpot fogging the windows. Amelie seldom had the opportunity to fix dinner. But today was her day off; she had planned this in advance.

Benjamin was quiet all through the meal. He didn't pay attention to the food, ate mechanically, frowned around his fork.

She put on the kettle for coffee, brooding.

It was that woman, Amelie knew, the one who had come looking for John—the one who had driven Benjamin home. She had said something to him; she was on his mind. Amelie wanted to ask what this was all about, but she was scared of seeming jealous. Of seeming not to trust him. Maddeningly, Benjamin didn't talk about it either. His silence was so substantial it was like an item of clothing, a strange black hat he had worn into the house. She tried to negotiate around it, to accommodate herself to his mood . . . but it was too obvious to really ignore.

She stacked the dishes and put Bon Jovi on the stereo. The tape-player part still worked, but Roch's little two-step had twisted the tonearm off its bearings. Amelie hoped Benjamin wouldn't notice. She didn't want to tell him about Roch.

The truth was that Amelie didn't feel too secure about men in general. She imagined that if she had a shrink this was the kind of thing she would confess to him. *I don't feel too secure about men.* It was one of those things you can know about yourself, but knowing doesn't make it better. Maybe this was because of her shitty adolescence, her absentee father—who knew what? On TV these problems always had neat beginnings and tidy, logical ends. In life, it was different. The time when she came here from Montreal with Roch—that was an example.

It's funny, she thought, you say a word like *prostitution* and it sounds truly horrifying. Like "AIDS" or "cancer." But she had never thought of it that way when she was doing it. She met a couple of other girls who had been on the street a long time and they talked about hooking or turning tricks, but those words didn't apply, either. Not that she was too good for it: it was just that her mind veered away from the topic. She was *surviving.* Being paid for sex . . . it just wasn't something you thought much about, before or during or after. And when you stop doing it, you don't *have* to think about it. And so it goes away. It doesn't show. No visible scars . . . although sometimes, in her paranoid moments, Amelie wasn't so sure about that. Sometimes she developed the urge to hide her face when she rode the buses or waited on tables.

But by and large it was something she could forget about, and that was why Roch had pissed her off so intensely. *Reminding* her of that. Worse, acting like it was something she might do again.

As if, once you do it, you're never any better than that: it's what you *are*. Trained reflex. Go fetch. Lie down and roll over.

But really, that was just Roch. Roch always had a hard time figuring out what anybody else was doing or thinking. One time, when he was nine or ten, Roch asked a friend of Amelie's named Jeanette how come she was so ugly. Jeanette turned brick red and slapped his face. Roch wasn't hurt, his feelings weren't hurt, but he was almost comically surprised. Later he asked Amelie: what happened? Did he break a rule or something?

All Roch wanted was a little cash, a loan. He hadn't meant anything by it.

She was too sensitive, that was all.

What was *really* frightening was the question of how Roch might respond to the beating John had given him. Because, the thing was, Roch could not forget a humiliation. He harbored grudges and generally tried to pay them back with interest.

But, Amelie told herself, there was no point in dwelling on it now.

She dried the dishes, put the towel up to dry, joined Benjamin in the main room. The TV was a black-and-white model Amelie had bought from a thrift shop, attached to a bow-tie antenna from a garage sale. The rooming house didn't have cable, so they watched sitcoms on the CBC all evening. Benjamin didn't say a word—just folded his hands in his lap and seemed to watch, though his eyes were foggy and distracted. Sometime around midnight, they went to bed.

————

She was almost asleep, lying on her back in the dark room listening to the sound of the rain against the window, when he said:

"What if I went away for a while?"

She felt suddenly cold.

She sat up. "Where would you go?"

He shrugged. "I don't want to talk about that part of it."

Everything seemed in sudden high relief: the faint streetlight against the cloth curtains, the coolness of the bedsheets where they touched her thighs. "Is it connected with this woman?"

Saying it out loud at last.

He said, "She's a doctor."

"Are you sick?"

"Maybe."

"Is it about—" Another taboo. "About John?"

He nodded in the darkness, a shadow.

Amelie said, "Well, I don't want you to leave."

"But if I have to?"

"I don't know what that means—'have to.' If you have to, then you just do it."

"I mean, would you be here for me."

His voice was solemn, careful.

"I don't know," she said. Thinking: Christ, yes, of *course* I'll be here! He was the best thing in her life and if there was even a chance of him coming back . . . but she couldn't say that. "Maybe," she said.

He nodded again.

He said, "Well, maybe it won't happen."

"Talk to me," she said. "Before you do anything."

"I'll try," Benjamin said.

And then silence. And the rain beating down.

––––––––

They woke a little after dawn and made love.

There was one frightening moment, when Amelie looked into his eyes, and for a second—not longer than that—she had the terrifying feeling that it was John looking down at her, his cold and penetrating vision a kind of rape . . . but then she blinked, and the world slid back into place; he was Benjamin again, moving against her with a passion that was also kindness and which she had allowed herself to think of as love.

The vision of him crowded out her fear.

He was Benjamin. And that was good.

7

For the rest of that rainy October week Susan immersed herself in the mystery of John Shaw.

I've talked to him, she thought. In a sense, I *know* him. . . .

But beyond that loomed the inescapable fact: *He is not entirely human.*

There was no way to reconcile these ideas.

She tried to stay in her hotel room in case he called, but by Thursday morning she was overcome with cabin fever. She left a firm order at the desk to take any phone messages and set out on foot with no real direction in mind.

The rain had stopped, at least. The sky was overcast and the wind was cold, but even that was gratifying after the monotony of recycled hotel air. She walked west, away from the downtown core. Toronto was a banking city, crowded with stark office towers; its charm, she had decided, was peripheral to this, in Chinatown or the University district. She turned north along University Avenue, willfully avoiding the direction of Benjamin's office. Shortly before noon she found herself between a phalanx of peanut carts and the granite steps of the Royal Ontario Museum, with pennies in her pocket and nowhere else to go.

Inside, the museum was all high domed ceilings and Egyptiana, botanical displays and gemstones under glass. Susan appreciated these, but she especially liked the dark vaults of the dinosaur arcade, cool Pleistocene fluorescence and faint voices like the drip of water. The articulated bones of Triceratops regarded her with the stately indifference of geological time. Susan returned the look for almost a quarter of an hour, reverently.

Beyond Triceratops, the corridor wound away to the left. She eased back slowly into human history; where she was startled, turning a corner, by the Evolution of Man.

It was one of those museum displays that compare the skull sizes, tools, curvature of the spine across the eons. Here was Homo habilis leading the human march out of Olduvai, but surely, Susan thought, the entire concept was archaic: did anyone still believe evolution had proceeded in this reasonable arc? From stone club to Sidewinder missile, here at the pinnacle of time?

But she supposed John would have had a place here, too, if anyone had known about him. Dr. Kyriakides had once told her that he wanted to engineer the next step in human evolution. "A *better* human being. One who would make us obsolete. Or at least embarrass us for our vices."

So here would be John, leading the march toward the future, a little taller and a little brighter and in his hand—what? A pocket H-bomb? A neutrino evaporator? Or he might be as pristine as Dr. Kyriakides had envisioned him . . . as weaponless and innocent as a child.

She turned away. Suddenly she wanted the high ceilings of the main arcades, not this cloistered space. But before she left she paused before the diorama of Neolithic Man, stooped and feral in wax, wincing at the first light of human awareness. Our father, she thought. Mine and John's, too; as obdurate, inscrutable, and foreign as every father is.

————

Still he did not call.

Friday afternoon she phoned Maxim Kyriakides at his office at the University.

He said, "I should have come myself. Forced the issue. Then he could not have avoided me."

"I don't think that's what he needs. That is—I had the impression—it would have made things worse."

"You may be right. Still, I could come there if necessary." He added, "I suppose I'm feeling guilty about demanding so much of your time."

"It's all right."

"Is it really? You weren't so obliging when you began the project. I had to talk you into leaving."

"I think it's different now—meeting him and all. I wasn't sure what to expect. Some kind of monster."

"Are you sure he's not?"

She was quietly shocked. "I don't know what you mean."

"Only that it's easy to forget that he is what he is. He has abilities you won't have encountered. His point of view is unique. He may not feel bound by conventional behavior."

"I understand that."

"Do you really, Susan? I hope so. I worry that you might be projecting your own concerns onto him. That would be a mistake."

"I know." (But she was blushing.) "There's no danger of that."

"Then I'm sorry I mentioned it." He was being very Old World now, very charming. "I really do appreciate the work you're doing, Susan."

She thanked him—cautiously.

He said, "Stay as long as you like. But keep in touch."

"I will."

"And ultimately—if there's nothing we *can* do—"

"I know," she said. "I'm prepared for that."

She was lying, of course.

———

Benjamin called that evening. The call was brief, but Susan could hear the anxiety in his voice.

"There's a problem," he said.

"What is it? Is it John? Is he sick?"

Cold night and the city bright but impersonal beyond the windows.

"He's thinking of leaving town," Benjamin said. "You want the truth? I think he's afraid of you."

"We have to talk," Susan said.

———

She met him at an all-night cafeteria on Yonge Street.

The club next door was hosting a high-powered reggae band; the bass notes came pulsing through the wall. Susan ordered coffee and drank it black.

Benjamin came in from the street shivering in his checkerboard flannel jacket. She marveled again at how unlike John he was: nothing to distinguish this man from anyone else on the street. He smiled as he pulled up his chair, but the smile was perfunctory.

He shucked his jacket and ordered a coffee. He added cream and sugar, sipped once, said: "Oh—hey, that's good. I needed that."

"You look tired."

"I am. Ever since we had our talk . . . I guess I'm kind of reluctant to fall asleep. Don't know who'll wake up. He wants more time, Susan. All of a sudden he's fighting me."

"I didn't know he had a choice."

"You come to terms with something like this. But there was never any real conflict before. I mean, you don't understand what it's like. It's not something you think about if you can help it. You just live your life. I think . . . John was fading because he didn't really care anymore. He let me do what I wanted and he wasn't around much. Now . . . this whole thing has stirred him up."

Susan leaned forward across the table. "You can tell that?"

"I feel him wanting to be awake." Benjamin sat back in his chair, regarding her. "You think that's a good thing, don't you?"

"Well, I—I mean, it's important to know—"

"I had to take a couple of days off." Benjamin smiled ruefully. "John was kind enough to phone in sick for me."

"You said he was thinking about going away?"

"Both of us have been. I talked to Amelie about it. I asked her if it would be okay, you know, if I didn't see her for a while."

"What did she say?"

"Basically, that it would be okay, but it wouldn't make her happy." He took a compulsive gulp of coffee. "If we do this—if we go for treatment—would it be possible for Amelie to come along? There's not much to keep her here. I mean, budget permitting and all."

"I'd have to talk to Dr. Kyriakides. It may be possible." She hoped not. But that was petty. "You were saying about John—"

"John's pulling in the opposite direction. I don't usually have much access to his thoughts, you know, but some things come through. He's thinking of leaving, but not for treatment. He wants to hit the road. Get out of town. Run away."

"From me?"

"From this doctor of yours. From the *situation*. But yes, you're a part of it. I think you disturbed him a little bit. There's something about you that worries him."

"What? I don't understand!"

Benjamin shrugged. "Neither do I."

"You think there's a chance he'll really do it?"

"Leave? I don't know. I really don't. Maybe, if he panics. This is all new territory for me, you know. It's hard to explain, but . . . I was just getting used to living a life. I mean, I know what I am.

I'm a shadow. I'm aware of that. I was always a shadow. I'm something he made up. But I look around, I have thoughts, I see things—I'm as alive as you are." He shook his head. "I don't want to go back to the way it was before. You know what I like, Susan? I like the sunshine. I like the light." His gaze was very steady and for a moment he *did* remind her of John. "So is that why you're here? To send me back into the shadows?"

Susan inspected the Formica tabletop. "No. No one wants that."

"Because you're right. There *is* something happening to us. Something *up here.*" He tapped his head. "I can feel it. Like the boundaries are loosening up. Things are stirring around. And I don't know where that's taking me." He added, "I have to admit I'm a little bit scared."

Susan took his hand. "Both of you need help. We have to make sure both of you get it."

"The thing is, I don't know if I can do that. I'll do what I can. Whatever happens, I'll try to keep in touch. I'll let you know where we are. But I'm not in charge here. It's not my choice."

"Tell me what I can do."

"I don't know." He smiled wearily. "Probably nothing."

8

Tony Morriseau was hanging out at the corner of Church and Wellesley minding his own business when he saw the Chess Player coming toward him.

Actually, *stalking* him was more like it. This was unusual, and Tony regarded the Chess Player's lanky figure with a faint, first tremor of unease.

Tony knew the Chess Player from the All-Nite Donut Shop on Wellesley. Tony had never spoken to him, but the guy was a fixture there, poised over his board like a patient, predatory animal. Hardly anybody ever played him. Certainly not Tony. Tony wasn't into games. His experience was that the Chess Player didn't talk and nobody talked to the Chess Player.

Still, Tony recognized him. Tony was a quarter Cree on his mother's side and liked to think he had that old Indian thing, keeping his ear to the ground. Tony made most of his money—which was not really a lot—selling dope out of the back of his '78 Corvette, parked just down the block. His profit margins weren't high and his only steady customers were the local gay trade and some high school kids. Still, Tony was a fixture on the street; he had been here since '84. Same Corvette, same business. He told himself it was only temporary. He wanted to make significant money, and this—dealing in streetcorner volume at a pathetic margin, from a supplier who had been known to refer to Tony as "pinworm"—this wasn't the way to do it. He would find something else. But until then . . .

Until then it was business as usual—and what did this geek want from him, anyhow?

Tony pressed his back against a brick wall and gave the Chess Player a cautious nod. The evening traffic rolled down Church Street under the lights; an elderly Korean couple strolled past, heads down in abject courtesy. Tony looked at the Chess Player, now directly in front of him, and the Chess Player stared back. Big deep hollow eyes, round head, burr haircut. He made Tony distinctly nervous. Tony said, "Do I know you?"

"No," the Chess Player said. "But I know you. I want to buy something."

"Maybe I don't have anything to sell."

The Chess Player reached into his pocket and pulled out a roll of bills. He peeled a fifty off the top and stuffed it into the pocket of Tony's down vest. Tony's heart began to pump faster, and it might have been the money but it might also have been the look on the guy's face. He thought: Am I afraid? And thought: Fuck, no. Not me.

He transferred the bill to his hip pocket. "So what is it you want?"

"Amphetamines," the Chess Player said, and Tony was briefly amused at how dainty he made it sound: am*phet*amines.

"How many?"

"How many have you got?"

Tony did a little mental calculation. He began to feel better. "Come with me," he said.

Down the block to the Corvette. Checking the guy out sideways as they walked. Tony kept most of his stock in the back of the 'Vette. He had been ripped off twice; and while that was something you expected—he was not a volume dealer and he could eat the occasional losses—it was also something you didn't want to set yourself up for. But Tony was fairly smart about people (his Cree instinct, he told himself), and he didn't believe the Chess Player was a thief. Something else. Something strange, maybe something a little bit dangerous. But not a thief.

Tony opened the car door and rooted out a Ziploc bag of prescription pharmaceuticals from the space under the driver's seat. He held the bag low inside the angle of the door, displaying it to the buyer but not to the public. "Some of these suit your fancy?"

"All of them."

"That would be—you'd be talking some serious money there."

He named a price and the Chess Player peeled off the bills. Large money amounts and no haggling. It was like a dream. Tony stuffed the cash into his rear pocket, a tight little bulge. He could go home. He could have a drink. He was prepared to celebrate.

But the Chess Player leaned in toward him and said, very quietly and calmly, "I want the car, too."

Tony was too startled to react at once. The Corvette! It was his only real possession. He had bought it from a retired dentist in Mississauga for a fraction of what it was worth. Put some money into it. The fiberglass body had been through some serious damage, but that was purely cosmetic. Under the hood, it was mainly original numbers. "Fuck, man, you can't have my car—that's my *car*."

But it came out like a whine, a token protest, and Tony realized with a deep sense of shock that he *was* afraid of this man; it was just that he could not say exactly why.

Big, almost luminous eyes peering into his. Christ, Tony thought, he can see right through me!

Without blinking, the Chess Player pulled out his roll of bills again.

Tony stared at the cash as it came off the roll. It was like a machine at work. Crisp new money. He counted up to $5000; then—without thinking—he said, "Hey, look, I paid less than that for it . . . it needs bodywork, you know?"

The Chess Player put the money in Tony's vest pocket. The touch of his fingers there was weirdly disturbing. "Buy a new car," the Chess Player said. "Give me the keys."

Be damned if Tony didn't do just that. Handed them over without a word. Mysterious.

He would spend a lot of long nights wondering about it.

The Chess Player was about to climb in and drive away when Tony shook his head—it was like waking up from a bad dream into a hangover—and said, "Hey! My *property!*"

"Take what you want," the Chess Player said.

Panicking, Tony retrieved ten ounces of seeded brown marijuana and a milk carton of Valium and stuffed them hastily into a brown paper A&P bag.

The door slammed closed as the Corvette pulled away.

He watched as the automobile faded into the night traffic, southbound on Church, all the while thinking to himself: What was that? Jesus Christ almighty!—what *was* that?

John Shaw stopped off at the apartment to pack a change of clothes and leave a note.

Within ten minutes he had folded every useful item into two denim shoulderbags, including the bulk of the money he had withdrawn from his private accounts. The note to Amelie was more difficult.

He hesitated over pen and paper, thinking about the man who had sold him the Corvette.

He wasn't proud of what he'd done. It was a skill he had mastered a long time ago, a finely honed vocabulary of body and voice. With the right gestures and the necessary words, he could intimidate almost anyone—play the primate chords of fear, anger, love, or distaste, and do so at will. For a time, when his contempt for humanity had reached its zenith, he did it often. It was a means to an end, as irrelevant to ethical considerations as the shearing of a sheep.

Or so he had thought.

That time had passed; but he was pleased by the outcome of the little experiment he had just performed on Tony Morriseau. Old skills intact. So much had been lost, obscured by unconsciousness. But maybe not permanently.

He had been asleep. Now he was awake.

He wrote:

Must leave. Try to understand.

He wondered how much more he ought to say. He could summon up Benjamin long enough to compose a more serious message. Could even play at being Benjamin without invoking the real, or potent, Benjamin. But he was reluctant to do that now . . . it was a mistake he had made too often before.

He debated signing Benjamin's name, then decided it would be more honest, and possibly kinder, not to. In the end he simply hung the note (two sentences, five words) on the kitchen cupboard.

Hurrying to escape these small, crowded rooms.

———

The Corvette protested only a little when he nosed it onto the expressway and into the light midnight traffic northbound out of the city. He had been awake for two days now and some of the old clarity had come back to him. He was able to read the condition of the Corvette's engine through the grammar of its purrs and hesitations, and his sense was that the vehicle was old but basically sound. Something catastrophic might happen, a crack in the engine block or an embolism in an oil line; but the pistons were turning over neatly, the gears meshed, the brakes were clean. With any luck, the car would get him where he was going.

The rain that had hovered over the province for the last two weeks had finally drifted off eastward. It was a clear, cold night. Between the glaring road-lights—growing sparse out here in farm territory—he was able to see a scatter of stars. He had always liked looking at the stars and sometimes felt a special connection with them, in their isolation in the dark sky. It was the kinship he felt for all lost, strange, and distant things.

The road arrowed up a long incline, an ancient glacial moraine, and suddenly the stars were right in front of him. Impulsively, he edged the Corvette's gas pedal down. It was long past midnight and nothing was moving here but a heavily freighted lumber truck. He took the Corvette past it in an eyeblink. A brief taste of diesel through the cracked wing window, then onward. He watched the speedometer creep up. At eighty-five mph the Corvette was showing some of its age and neglect. He read a whiff of hot metal and oil, the spark plugs burning themselves clean.

He liked this—the farms and empty autumn fields blurring behind him; the sense of motion. But more than that. It was a private pleasure, uniquely his own. His reflexes and his sense of timing seldom came up against their inherent limits; it was exhilarating to push that envelope a little. He was very far from those limits even now—the speedometer still inching upward—but he was attentive, focused, and energized. Every shiver of the chassis or tremor of the road became significant information, raw data flooding him. He came up fast on a sixteen-wheel Mayflower truck and passed it, left the trucker's horn screaming impotently down a corridor of cold night air.

This was a world only he was fit to inhabit, he thought, this landscape of speed and reflex. For anyone else it would be next door to death. For John it was a sunny meadowland through which his thoughts ran in a cool, rapid cascade.

There was a shimmy now from the rear end of the Corvette.

And he would have to slow down soon in any case, or risk running some radar trap or pushing the engine past its tolerances. In any case, it was time to fill the gas tank. But he allowed himself one moment more. This fine intoxication.

He was beginning to ease back on the gas pedal when the Corvette fishtailed coming around a slow curve.

He was on top of it instantly, manhandling the wheel, feeling the sudden change from vehicular momentum to deadly inertia. There was a long spin on the cool night pavement, tire treads fraying and screaming as the rear end wheeled around and the car tottered, wanting to turn over. John held onto the steering wheel, focused into this long moment . . . working with the car's huge momentum, tugging it back from the brink, correcting and correcting again as the tires etched long V's and W's on the dark pavement.

He had the Corvette under control within microseconds. A moment later it was motionless on the shoulder of the road.

Sudden silence and the ticking of the hot engine. Wind in a dark October marsh off to the right of him.

A shiver of relief ran up his spine.

He looked at his hand. It was shaking.

He opened the glove compartment, tugged out the Ziploc bag, rolled an amphetamine cap into his mouth.

He dry-swallowed the pill and angled the car slowly back onto the highway, carefully thinking now about nothing at all.

––––––

Fundamentally, it was a question of past and future.

He took the first car ferry of the morning across Georgian Bay to the northern shore of Lake Superior. The North Shore was a stark landscape of pine and rock and the brittle blue Superior horizon. Gas station towns, souvenir stands, Indian reservations; black bear and deer in the outback. During the last world war, captive German military officers had been assigned logging duty in this wilderness. There were places, John understood, where their K-ration tins lay rusting under the pine needles and the washboard lumber roads. In summer the highway would have been crowded with tourists; but it was late in the year now and the campgrounds were vacant and unsupervised. He drove all day through the cold, transparent air; after nightfall he turned down a dirt track road to an empty campsite near the lakeshore. He zipped up his insulated windbreaker and stoked a kindling fire in one of the brick-lined barbecue pits. When he had achieved a satisfactory blaze he added on windfall until the fire was roaring and crackling. Then he settled back to rising sparks and stars and the lonely sound of Lake Superior washing at the shore. The fire warmed his hands and face; his back was cold. He heated a can of soup until the steam rose up in the wintery air.

When the meal was finished, he sat in the car with the passenger door opened toward the fire, thinking about the past and the future.

The past was simple. He contained it. He contained it in a way no other human being could contain it, as a body of mnemonic experience he could call up at will—his life like an open book.

Excepting the chaos of his earliest infancy, there was not a day of his life that John could not instantly evoke. He had divided his life into three fundamental episodes—his time with Dr. Kyriakides, his time with the Woodwards, his time as an adult. Four, if you counted the recent re-emergence of Benjamin as a new and distinct epoch. And each category was a vast book of days, of autumns and winters and summers and springs, each welling from its own past and arrowing toward its own future with a logic that had always seemed incontrovertible.

Until now. For most of his life he had been running toward the future as if it contained some sort of salvation. In the last few years, mysteriously, that had changed. The future, he thought, was a promise that might not be kept. Now he was running . . . not quite aimlessly, because he had a destination in mind; not toward the past, precisely; but toward a place where his life had taken a certain turn. A fork in the road. Maybe it would be possible to retrace his steps, turn the other way; this time, maybe, toward a genuine future, an authentic light.

He recognized the strong element of rationalization in this. Self-deception was a vice he had never permitted himself. But there comes a time when your back is to the wall. So you follow an instinct. You do what you have to.

A sudden, bitter wind came off the lake. The fire was dying. He banked the embers and then shut himself into the car, blinking at the darkness and afraid to sleep. He looked longingly at the glove compartment, picturing the bag of pills there. But he had to pace himself. He felt the fatigue poisons running through his body. No choice now but to sleep.

Anyway—he would need the pills more, later.

He watched the stars until the windows clouded with the vapor of his breath. Finally, with an almost violent suddenness, he slept.

He drove west into the broad prairie land.

Coming through Manitoba he ran into a frontal system, rain and wet snow that sidelined the Corvette in a little town called Atelier while the Dominion Service Station and Garage replaced the original tires with fresh snow-treads. John checked into a motel called The Traveller and picked up some books at the local thrift shop.

Entertainment reading for the post-human: a science-fiction novel; *The Magic Mountain* (the only Mann he'd never looked into); a paperback bestseller. Also a battered Penguin edition of Olaf Stapledon's *Odd John*—the joke, of course, was on himself.

He had read the Stapledon many times before. It was a classic of English eccentric writing of the thirties, the story of a mutant supergenius born to ordinary humanity. During his adolescence John had adopted the book as a kind of bible. The story was fuzzy-minded, uneven, sometimes silly in its literal-mindedness; but he felt a resonance with Odd John's sense of "spiritual contamination" by mankind, his "passion of loneliness." The John of the book sought out others of his kind—telepaths and mutants—and founded a utopian colony which the Great Powers ultimately destroyed. Two unlikely assumptions there, John thought: that there *were* others of his kind, and that such people would constitute a perceptible threat to anyone.

But the biggest mistake Stapledon had made, John thought, was his character's self-sufficiency. Stapledon compared his Odd John to a human being among apes. But a human being raised by apes isn't a superior ape. In all the qualities that matter to apes, he's not much of an ape at all. And if he feels contemptuous of the apes, it's only the automatic contempt of the rejected outsider.

Still—in this desolate prairie town—some of that contempt came welling up.

After dinner he went walking along the narrow main street of Atelier where the Trans-Canada passed through. Atelier was a grain town; its landmarks were a railway depot, a Chinese restaurant, and a five and dime. Nobody much was out in the weather except for a few sullen leather-jacketed teens occupying the Pizza Patio. He pressed through the sleet beyond the local mall and discovered signs of life at a tiny sports arena. An illuminated Port-A-Sign announced:

> *REV HARMON BELWEATHER*
> *REVIVAL TONIGHT 9:00*
> *MIRACLES!*
> *HEALING!*

John gazed awhile at the sign; then—curious, sad, and entirely alone—he joined the small crowd in the overheated lobby, indoors and away from the rain.

———

The auditorium was three-quarters full when the ushers closed the doors.

It was an elderly crowd, with a few earnest young couples scattered around the arena. He counted several wheelchairs, a great many crutches. A woman in a gingham skirt moved down the aisles, stopping here and there to exchange a few words with the audience. She paused at the row in front of John and chatted with a hugely overweight man about his gall bladder troubles. She caught John's glance and moved toward him; when he did not look away she asked, "Are you here for healing?"

He shook his head in the negative.

"Are you sure? You look like a man with a need."

He gave her a long, focused look. The woman in the gingham dress tugged at her earlobe, stared a moment longer, then shrugged uneasily and moved away.

The audience hushed as the lights dimmed. A local choir performed a hymn, and then Reverend Belweather took the stage. He was a squat, compactly fat man in a sincere Republican suit. His hair was cut to Marine length; he wore rings on his fingers. He began in a low-key fashion, whispering into the hand mike—you had to strain forward to hear him—but he was good, John thought. He read the crowd well and he was good with his body, with his aggressive strut and upraised palm. He preached to the crowd for forty minutes under the fierce klieg lights, rising to thunderous crescendos of damnation and salvation, the sweat rivering off the slope of his forehead. John closed his eyes and felt the crowd around him as a single, physical thing—an animal, aroused to some terrible confusion of eroticism and fear. The human odor was as physical as heat in the confined space of the auditorium and it beat against him like a pulse. I pity them, John thought. And I hate myself for my pity. And I hate them for provoking it.

Wishing, at the same time, that he could be a part of it. He understood the profound comfort here. To be not alone. But he could not wholly grasp the beatitude beneath this stink of human sweat. He had read too much history. It smelled like Torquemada and his chambers; it smelled like Belsen and the killing fields of Cambodia.

The healing came last. Reverend Belweather called up the afflicted by name or disorder. "God informs me there's a Michael among us . . . Michael with a gall bladder!" And the fat man in the forward aisle stood up and ambled toward the stage, shocked into obedience.

Obscure in the shadows, John followed him down.

An experiment.

He stood in this cluster of diseased, dying, and broken individuals and felt a second wave of paralyzing contempt. Contempt for their sheeplike vulnerability; contempt for the man who was shearing them. I hate them, he thought, for *cooperating* in this . . . for their stupidity, he thought; because I cannot forgive them for it.

The healing act itself was anticlimactic, a tepid discharge of the tensions that filled the auditorium. A hand on the forehead, the hot breath of blessing, the command to shed those crutches and walk—at least as far as the wings, where the Reverend Belweather's muscular stage crew redistributed the crutches and wheelchairs as needed. The woman in the gingham dress lingered there, also.

John edged his way to the stage.

Reverend Belweather regarded him with a certain amount of suspicion—this odd bird among the flock—and said, "Quickly, son, what exactly is your ailment?"

"I have a headache," John said.

Reverend Belweather turned his eyes toward heaven, as much exasperation as prayer in the look. "Dear God," he said to the microphone, "we join together in begging an end to this young man's discomfort." And the hand on the head.

Reverend Belweather's hand was fleshy and moist. John imagined something pale and unwholesome, a dead thing touching him.

He concentrated for a moment. He could not say why this impulse had overtaken him. Some marriage of cruelty and distaste. One more experiment; there had been many before. But there was no restraining it.

Reverend Belweather yanked his hand away from John's head as he felt the skin writhing there.

Spontaneous scars and wounds that appear in a religious trance are called "stigmata." The phenomenon occurs in faiths from Catholicism to Voodoo; an interaction between mind and body triggered by religious ecstasy.

John was able to do it at will.

Reverend Belweather stared with horror at the cross of raised, feverish skin that had formed on John's forehead.

He managed, "Who *are* you?"

"It doesn't matter," John said. "What matters is that your wife has a radio transmitter built into her hearing aid and that you're using it to defraud these people. You're in violation of three federal statutes and you're committing a sin. You should cancel tomorrow's performance."

Reverend Belweather staggered back as if the floor had shifted under his feet. He looked for his stage crew—the big men in the wings. They had already sensed a ripple in the flow and moved forward. "Get him the fuck out of here," the Reverend Harmon Belweather said, his voice suddenly shrill and petulant. "Just get him the fuck out—*now!*" But he had clutched the hand-mike to his chest in an involuntary spasm of panic, and the words rang and echoed through the big Tannoy P.A. speakers like an invocation, or a failed and panicky exorcism.

It had been, of course, a stupid and dangerous thing to do. John turned and merged into the crowd of the crippled and the ill as the Reverend Belweather's henchmen advanced. They were large but slow and they hadn't had a good look at him; he was out a rear door and into the cold rain before they realized he was gone.

He arrived back at the motel wet, cold, and rank with amphetamine sweat, but the girl behind the desk smiled at him as he passed; and the smile provoked an old response. He stopped and turned to face her. Eighteen or maybe nineteen years old, broad bones, an aggressive blur of lipstick. And that smile. She returned his look. "318, right?"

His room number. He nodded. "You were here when I checked in."

"Right, that's right. I'm on till midnight. Shift's just about up."

He watched her eyes and her lips. The smile was tentative but provocative, an offer half made. He surmised that she had allowed guests to come on to her in the past and that she had mixed feelings about it, guilt colored with arousal; that she liked him because he looked a little dangerous coming in hollow-eyed from the rain; that she was scared of him, too, a little.

The possibility was tantalizing. She was a sheep, a goat, an ape, a human animal—but I'm human too, he thought, from the neck down. She shouldn't have provoked him with that smile. Nobody ever smiled at him. The rain and the tension had disguised some obvious clue to his nature: *she doesn't recognize the devil.* Horns and tail don't show in this light. Reverend Belweather, I am a stronger persuader than you are.

It was as easy as asking. Easy as buying a used Corvette. Look deep into my eyes and see precisely what you want, a tall westbound stranger with no attachments and big hands, see our dovetailed needs. He took her to his room and undressed her in the dark, pronouncing the words she wanted so desperately to hear, disguising himself so that she would not recoil and leave. Dangerous, this eager merging of skin and skin, sudden loss of surface tension; this knocking loose of props inside him until, delirious with orgasm and fatigue, he was no longer sure who or where he was. After a time she stood and dressed in the faint light —the light that comes through motel windows in prairie towns on cold nights after midnight—a glimmer of wet on her thigh, and

John was startled by the immediacy of the vision (or was it a symptom of his decline?), the absolute solidity of white shoulder and cascade of hair. A sudden longing radiated through him like a pulse. She turned toward him momentarily and he waited for the revulsion in her eyes, her dawning sense of his alienness, but there was none: only a flicker of curiosity. She smiled. "Who's Susan?"

John sat up on the bed, wordless.

"You said her name. I guess you didn't even know it. Girl-friend? Wife? Well, it doesn't matter."

He managed, "I'm sorry."

"No, I'm flattered. You must love her a lot."

She left him staring at the door.

Sleeping, he dreamed of his first sexual encounter.

He was sixteen and he had abandoned Benjamin and he was about to abandon the Woodwards; as an experiment, he seduced a female classmate. He selected his target and approached her methodically. She was a fragile bundle of neuroses and exposed nerves, therefore easy to manipulate. Which he did: he flattered and provoked and humiliated her into a motel bedroom, and he fucked her there—there was no other word for it. He obtained her passive submission and he fucked her.

Was it satisfying?

On the most elementary level, yes, it was. As an experiment, it was wholly successful. Fucking this schoolgirl in the dark was a confirmation of everything he had learned about himself, about his superiority. She was a lesser creature, which rendered any ethical objections moot. The sin, if there was a sin here, was not rape but bestiality, surely excusable under the circumstances.

Two things bothered him, however, and made him reluctant to repeat the experiment.

The first was that, while he was with her, while he was hovering at the brink of orgasm, some subterranean and scary impulse caused him to mouth the words "I love you" against her ear. She hadn't noticed, thank God. But it troubled John immensely. The words weren't his words! And words were his environment: words were where he lived. If this brick could collapse, how secure was the structure he had made of his life?

The second disturbing thing was the way she looked at him when they were finished. He switched on the bedside lamp and began to dress. He turned and caught her eyes fixed on him, and the expression on her face was one of silent shock: *What am I doing here? Christ, what have I done?*

He recognized the look.

He hated it.

It was far too familiar.

When he awoke it was five-fifteen of the next evening and the last daylight was bleeding away in a steely grey sky.

He checked out at the desk. There was another woman at the counter, middle-aged, lumpily overweight. She smiled and totaled his bill. "Late to be leaving," she observed. "Are you one of those night drivers?"

He nodded.

"Yeah," she said, "we get a few of those. Some people prefer it. Me, I think it's lonely going down the highway all by yourself in the dark. Oh well . . . I guess people are different that way."

He looked at the bill. "What's this charge?"

"Why, that's your phone call. Long distance to Toronto about 11 A.M. this morning. You came in the office and asked me how to get a line out, and I—hey, mister, is something wrong? What's the matter—you don't *remember?*"

In the Corvette he swallowed two pills and washed them down with coffee from a thermos, then gunned the engine and sailed west.

He passed the arena on his way out of Atelier. According to the billboard, the Reverend Belweather had canceled for tonight.

———

There was fresh-fallen snow in the Rockies but the roads were clear. The Corvette labored up and through a world of pine and snow and rock and cold blue sky; he was closing in on his objective now. John especially did not want to sleep—the sleep might revive his twin, if only momentarily, as it had in Atelier—and so he began to rely on the amphetamines when he felt fatigue settling in. This effectively killed his appetite, which in turn eliminated restaurant stops and saved a little time, though he did periodically force himself to stop for food. He was running the physical machine hard and he was conscious of the dangers that imposed.

He was careful; but even so, coming down the slope of the Rockies into coastal British Columbia, he began to hallucinate.

Rockfaces and switchbacks took on a sinister, knife-sharp significance. One looming wall of granite, where the mountain had been blasted to accommodate the road, compressed itself into a sudden likeness of Maxim Kyriakides—the rugged features, fierce brows, flat gray eyes. Max as he had appeared to John as a child. This immense, this unshakable. Well, he thought, as Amelie might say, *Fuck you, Max.* Get thee behind me.

It was the pills, he thought. They were responsible for this, the eruption of metaphor into his visual field. He shook his head and worked hard at concentrating on the road.

Of course, he thought, it might be the dissolution that Susan Christopher had warned him about. The cortical locus of his ego, the John Shaw part of his brain, misfiring in the dark of the skull . . . as it had when he almost allowed the Corvette to cartwheel on the highway out of Toronto. But that was not an allowable thought.

Not yet.

He blinked away the mutant landscape and reached for his baggie of pills.

———

He abandoned the Corvette in the vast parking lot at Tsawassen, where the ferries left the mainland of British Columbia for the Gulf Islands.

It was a bright, clear autumn day. The ferry dock was at the end of a long artificial spit of land; the waiting room windows looked over the placid blue water. John stood in the sunlight watching as the Victoria ferry eased into dock. Peaceful here, but he was wound up with drug energy. Twitchy restlessness and fatigue poisons, strange little seretonin rushes from his overworked neurochemistry. He made his body calm, tried to suppress the raw-nerve tingling in his arms and legs. He thought of Susan Christopher.

The thought was unbidden but very strong. Another eruption out of his past, he thought, this one more recent. Another face. Well, he liked her face. He held it in his mind for a moment, and the influence was soothing. Her face was uncommonly revealing and it was possible to read every flicker of her psyche in it. Her timidity, of course, and her fear of him, and under that something else, a fresh grief . . . but these things did not define her. There was also an openness, a willfulness. Intelligence. And she liked him; she felt some connection with him.

A dim sexual urge fought through the amphetamine haze. But that was inappropriate . . . now and maybe forever. Sudden associative memories of old experiments, encounters in the dark. And this cynical, familiar thought: A man may be raised by apes. But does he *love* the apes?

In the blue Gulf water a ferry sounded its horn. John shouldered his knapsack and shuffled aboard.

The afternoon faded toward evening. Crossing the Gulf, standing alone on the windswept outer deck, he watched the peak of Mount Hood, ancient volcanic cinder cone, fading to red on the horizon.

He had come to Canada fifteen years ago. Memories of that time unreeled behind his eyes.

After he left the Woodwards, after a few years in transient jobs from Detroit to San Francisco, he decided he would be safer in Canada. Safer or, at least, harder to find. John understood certain facts about his past. He knew that his creation had been overseen by the American government in one of its more macabre incarnations—the CIA's MK-ULTRA or some related institution—and that this agency had lost interest in him shortly before he was delivered to the Woodwards. He was also aware that he was a potential embarrassment to these powerful people and that he would be safer if he could become anonymous. Canada seemed like a good place to do that.

Money had never been a problem. He was able to bluff his way into almost any kind of work. He paid for fabricated ID and began with a typesetting job in Vancouver. He put his savings into small, solid investments; he anticipated the city's urban growth cycles throughout the volatile 1970s and turned that insight into capital. He wasn't wealthy—wealth invites attention—but within a few years he was at least independent. For a time, his most permanent address had been a houseboat anchored on the North Shore. In the summers, when he could afford the time, he used the boat to explore the B.C. coastline.

Those journeys had satisfied his appetite for isolation, at least for a while. But it was an appetite that, once briefly whetted, began to grow beyond all bounds.

The ocean fed it. The ocean was indifferent, calm and vast. The ocean did not pay John Shaw any particular attention; the coastal rocks and piney inlets ignored his passage. There were places where he could land, come ashore, and move among the dark trees as quietly as the Haida or the Kwakiutl of a thousand years ago. The isolation was a new discovery for him, a thrilling one. Alone, he could become what he was meant to be: a new thing, a fresh creature on the earth.

In the spring of 1984 he had liquidated the bulk of his savings and bought property on one of the more obscure and inaccessible of the inhabited Gulf Islands, a chain of rocky prominences paralleling the inner coast of Vancouver Island. The smallest of these were unmapped rocks and shoals that disappeared with the tide; the one he came to think of as his own was hardly larger. The entire southern tip of this island was in effect his property: a domain; a kingdom, though he did not think of himself as its owner or ruler. He was its citizen—its subject. He had ransomed his savings for that privilege. There was enough money left to keep him in provisions, to pay for a cabin and a wind generator, for the books and the PC terminal he ferried in from the mainland.

Alone, he had immersed himself in cellular biology. He recognized the irony: he was adopting Max's specialty. But it was suddenly and overwhelmingly important to establish the link between himself and the rock pine, the sea otter, the sea itself. At the most basic level they were all very much alike, ribosomes and lysosomes, hydrogen and oxygen. Evolutionary history was inscribed into the substance of itself—organelles, once independent creatures, were imbedded in the cellular structure like the effigies of saints in the wall of a cathedral. Climbing among the shore rocks in late summer he observed blue-green algae in the glassy tide pools, prokaryotic cells, filaments of DNA floating free in the cytoplasm: primitive protein inventions. He handled shells washed up by storms, calciate rocks with the Fibonacci series imposed upon their shapes as if the clay itself had been possessed by mathematics.

This was the estate from which he had been disinherited. He was not even a genetic sport—the cells in his body, his DNA, were no more unusual than anyone's. His progeny, if he produced any, would not resemble him. Max had intervened after conception, in the womb; had performed chemical modifications that operated at the level of transcriptase and RNA, skewed protein messages carried through cellular reproduction in the zygote. In effect, his blueprints had been tampered with. Specifically, the protein code for the construction of a human forebrain had been altered; the basic human neural command—to build a more complex cerebrum—had been amplified. He was born with voluntary motor control and cutaneous sensation measurably greater than the norm. Other cortical functions—the generalized sensory threshold, language skills, abstract thought—registered beyond the curve of expectation as soon as they could be reasonably charted. By the age of five years he was way off scale on the Stanford-Binet intelligence test. He was "smart." He was also not entirely human.

He was not human, but he was protoplasm, and he guessed he had come to this isolated place to prove that to himself. We are all cast out from some kingdom, he thought. It was how the process worked. Chordates exiled from the world of the invertebrates, air-breathing vertebrates exiled from the sea. Mankind itself, cast out from the animal kingdom into the high, chilling air of self-awareness and the anticipation of personal mortality. I am not unique, he told himself. Merely alone.

It was a kind of consolation. But it had faded through the long winter and he was left with a growing sense of morbidity. Alone, he turned his attention to cellular pathology. He read research abstracts. He built an elaborate add-on memory system for his PC and tinkered with its program protocols until he could use it to generate elaborate models of metastatic 3LL carcinomas. He came to understand disease and aging as the agents of thermodynamic necessity—the spring of life unwinding on itself. The universe itself, he thought, was a broken symmetry in the unimaginable unmaterial from which it arose, an eruption of imperfection. And life was both a product of that process and a mirror of it. We carry our corruption from the womb, he thought. Max had believed in the perfectibility of mankind. But that was a superstition. Bad teleology and bad thermodynamics.

As time passed, he had traveled to the mainland less often.

When he did, he began to attract attention. His Levis were thin and sun-faded; he had grown a beard. He was astonished at his own reflection in the window of the night ferry to Tsawassen. Here was some feral creature, sun-darkened and wild-eyed . . . where was John Shaw?

What was John Shaw?

But he knew the answer. John Shaw was an invention—the lifework of Dr. Kyriakides.

How strange it must be, he thought, to create a human being— or a facsimile of one.

But I've done that, he thought. I *do* know what it's like.

He had invented Benjamin.

Waves of memory were triggered by the thought . . . memory, and the faint, disquieting sensation that something alive had moved inside him.

Coming back to this place now, it seemed as if he had never left.

He bought a week's rental on an aluminum motor launch from one of the larger islands, and made his way directly to the cabin, avoiding the main docks at the civilized end of the small island and beaching the boat in a rocky inlet. He secured the boat against the incoming tide and followed a crude path to the cabin from the shore.

The cabin hadn't changed much. The weather had pried up a few boards, and dry rot had taken out a corner of the porch stairs. A window was broken. Hikers had been here—he found a limp condom and the remains of a six-pack discarded in the back room. Forbidden pleasures. Violation and trespass. He swept all this away, down the back steps into the bushes. There was a small storage closet built into the rear of the cabin, which no one had bothered to loot; it contained mainly maintenance supplies and he was able to mend the broken window with a sheet of polyethylene.

Night was falling fast. John moved into the lengthening shadows of the pines beyond the cabin and gathered windfall for a fire. It had been a dry autumn and there was plenty of loose kindling. He startled a deer, which regarded him with wary eyes before it bolted into the bush.

He had a fire blazing in the stone fireplace before the sky was entirely dark, and enough kindling set aside to last the night. Come morning he would chop firewood. The weather was clear but very cold.

He rolled out his sleeping bag in front of the fire.

He was immensely tired.

He gave himself permission to sleep. Now, here, finally. But sleep wouldn't come. Strange how it was possible to be crazed with fatigue and still wide awake. Too many amphetamines, he thought, for far too long. He was still, on some level, speeding.

He wrapped himself in his down jacket and went outside, walking a few feet down a dark path to a slab of granite overlooking the water. He gazed at the cold, wholly transparent sky and listened to the rustle of dry leaves against the windward wall of the cabin. He felt his aloneness. And he understood—quite suddenly —that it was that once-glimpsed sense of connection that had brought him back here. The need—even if he was dying, especially if he was dying—to feel himself a part of something. If not humanity, then this. This stark, unforgiving, lovely night.

But there was nothing of him in this wilderness. He had expected to find at least an echo of himself, of his isolation, in sky and sea and stone; but the sky swallowed up his voice and the rock rejected his footprints.

He shuffled inside to wait for morning.

9

Amelie did her best to ignore the note on the kitchen cupboard. Problem was, it refused to go away.

She pretended it didn't exist. When she came home from the restaurant and found it, that first time, the note was like something washed up in a bottle: indecipherable and strange. *Must leave. Try to understand.* What did *that* mean? It didn't even look like Benjamin's writing.

He had talked about going away. True. But *this*—

It was too weird.

She washed the dishes. George had given her the evening off. She watched *Entertainment Tonight,* followed by a game show and a detective show. The images slid on past, video Valium. One day, she thought, we'll get cable. Then maybe there'll be something good to watch.

But the "we" made an odd hollow sound in her head.

She went to bed alone. Deep, brooding, dreamless sleep, and then she woke up—still alone. Well, that happened sometimes.

You couldn't predict with Benjamin. Obviously, he had problems. It was not as if he could entirely control . . . what he was.

She forced herself to make the trek to the bathroom, cold these mornings. She looked at herself in the mirror, naked and shivering, and she didn't like what she saw. Small breasts, pinpoint nipples, a mouse-brown thatch of pubic hair. A ratty little body, Amelie thought. Someone, probably Sister Madelaine from the École, had called her that. "Amelie, you are a ratty thing."

Ratty little me, Amelie thought.

She went to work without thinking about Benjamin.

It was an ordinary day at work, and that was good. She thought maybe she was projecting some kind of aura, because nobody bothered her much. Even her customers were polite—even George was polite. At the door, as she was leaving, he put his hand on her shoulder and said, "Are you okay?"

"Just a little down," Amelie said . . . regretting it instantly; because, in a strange way, saying so seemed to make it true.

"Some woman thing," George diagnosed.

Yeah, she thought, I'm getting my period. George could be such a moron sometimes. But he meant well. "Something like that."

"So cheer up," he said.

Thank you a whole lot for that terrific advice, Amelie thought.

She walked home in the cold dark. When she reached the apartment, the note was still attached to the cupboard.

She looked at it harder this time. Forced her eyes to track it. Blue Bic hieroglyphics. Really, what language *was* this?

And at the back of her head, where impossible thoughts were nevertheless sometimes pronounced, she heard:

I am alone now.

Oh, no.

Screw *that.* He'd be home. He would! It was only a matter of time.

She poked through the dresser drawers looking for something to smoke, something that would soothe her to sleep. This turned out to be a bad move, because she discovered that Benjamin's clothes had been pretty much cleared out. The vacant space was a signal to her, more comprehensible than the note and more final. This sad empty drawer. She slammed it shut. As it turned out, there was a joint hidden at the bottom of her purse—something she'd bought from Tony Morriseau a while back.

It got her stoned enough to enjoy a William Powell *Thin Man* movie coming fuzzily over the border from a network affiliate in Buffalo . . . but not so stoned that she didn't leap up from the sofa when the telephone rang. Benjamin, she thought, because it was late now and he must be thinking about her and who the hell else would be calling her at this hour?

Her hand trembled on the receiver. "Hello?"

But it wasn't Benjamin. It was Roch.

She couldn't understand him at first. He was speaking thick, muddled, obscene French. He's drunk, she thought. She said, in English, "What do you want?"

There was a long pause. "I need a place to stay."

"Oh, no . . . hey, come on, Roch, you know that's not a good idea."

"Oh, it *isn't? Isn't* it?"

Amelie wished she hadn't smoked. She felt suddenly feverish and sweaty. She felt her brother's attention focused on her like a heat-ray through the telephone.

"They fucking kicked me out of my apartment, Amelie. Non-payment. Bitch landlady calls me a deadbeat. You know? This . . . *toad*, with a dress like a burlap sack. Looks at me like I came out from a crack in the plaster. You are a deadbeat, she says, I'm locking you out. I told her, I have stuff in there. She says, you have *trash* in there and you can pick it up from the side of the road. I should have fucking killed her."

Amelie, who was tired of this, said, "So why didn't you?"

"Because she had some goddamnned pit bull or something on a

leash beside her. One of those killing dogs." He emitted a high, drunken laugh. "It even looked like her! But I should have . . . you know . . . I should have fucking *killed* her."

So do it sometime. Just do it, and then they'll lock you up and I won't have this problem.

She said, "There must be someplace you can stay."

It sounded like pleading.

"You're it," Roch said. "You're my sister. You owe this to me." He added, "What's the problem—that shithead you're living with? Well, you can just fucking ditch him. This is an emergency. I mean, I'm family, right? So tell him to get the hell out or I'll kick his ass."

You didn't have much luck last time you tried, Amelie thought —but then she remembered that Benjamin was gone. Maybe because she was stoned and frightened now, his absence became abruptly real. She really *was* alone here. All by herself in these broken-down rooms.

She didn't want to give in to Roch. But if she refused, odds were he'd be over here anyway. He would want a fight; and she couldn't face that . . . not now. . . .

So she told him, "Just tonight. Just until you find something. Okay? Just tonight."

He was instantly soothed. "That's my girl."

"I'm not your girl, Roch."

"You're there when I need you. That's what counts, right? That's what family is for."

"Sure. That's what family is for."

In the aftermath of his call, the silence in the room was stunning. She turned down the volume on the TV but she could still hear a high-pitched whine radiating from inside the set. A leaky tap ticked in the kitchen.

She turned away from the phone, then turned back as a flutter of motion attracted her eye. A slip of paper had been tucked under the phone; now it slipped to the floor. She picked it up and unfolded it.

A phone number. A name.

Susan Christopher.

The woman who had come looking for John Shaw.

Maybe Susan Christopher knows where Benjamin is, she thought. It was possible. But the Christopher woman might be out of town by now. Probably was. There was a hotel address written under the fold of the paper. Probably she would have checked out. Still—

No, Amelie instructed herself. Don't think about it now. Save it.

She tucked the note into her purse, down deep between her wallet and her make-up case—a safe place. She might want it, she thought. Later.

10

Susan stayed an extra month over schedule in Toronto, living frugally on the money Dr. Kyriakides had wired her and waiting for the phone to ring.

She developed a schedule. Her mornings were her own, and she used them to explore the city, on foot or by public transit. There was always the possibility that John might try to contact her during these hours, but it was a calculated risk: she could not simply sit in her room and wait. So she would wake up, shower, buy breakfast in the hotel coffee shop. She had left standing instructions with the switchboard to take her messages—which must have amused the telephone staff, since there *weren't* any messages, ever—and she was careful to get back no later than one o'clock in the afternoon, a stern rule that served to assuage her guilt.

In time, she developed a few favorite destinations. She liked riding the ferry to Ward's Island and back, Lake Ontario bleak and pretty in the November weather. She liked Chinatown. She discovered cheap, interesting lunches in the Vietnamese restaurants along Dundas west of University—John would approve, she thought. She shopped for reading material in the second-hand bookstores along the city's somewhat bohemian Queen Street strip. Afternoons, she would read by the phone. There were days when she spoke to no one except the waiter in the Saigon Maxima and the desk clerk at the hotel. The isolation had become a fact of her life. I am, she thought, like those people who live in caves for months on end. She had begun to lose any real sense of time.

It was Dr. Kyriakides who reminded her of how much time had truly passed. He phoned at the end of November and said, "I want you to come home now."

"But he hasn't called," Susan said. "He—"

"I think at this point we have to admit that it might not happen. When was the last time he contacted you? Almost a month ago, wasn't it?"

Approximately that. And it had been Benjamin, not John, and the news had not been encouraging—he was calling from a motel somewhere out west and he believed John was acting out some kind of regression, unwinding his life down the highway toward some unknown destination.

"But he said he'd try to call again," Susan protested. "If I leave now he won't be able to find us!"

"John can always find us if he wants to. That decision is in his hands. I suppose it always has been. We can't force our help on him. But my main concern, Susan, is you."

"I'm doing all right." But it sounded petulant, childish.

"You're becoming obsessive," Maxim Kyriakides said.

"Shouldn't I be? You're obsessive about John. You told me so."

"I have a legitimate reason. I'm entitled to my guilt, Susan. I've earned it."

She didn't want to explore the implications of that. "One more week."

"I don't see any point in prolonging the inevitable."

"I'll make you a deal. One more week, then I fly back—no arguments, no regrets."

Dr. Kyriakides was silent for a moment. "You know, you're not in a position to bargain."

"As a favor, then."

"Well . . . then let me make the arrangements. I'll buy you a flight back to O'Hare. One week from tonight. Precisely."

The thought of it was chilling. But he was right, of course; she couldn't stay here forever. She was living on his money, borrowing time against an academic career she could not postpone indefinitely. "All right," she said. The offer was generous, really. "Yes."

"Good. I'll call back when I have a flight number for you. You can pick up the ticket tomorrow."

––––––––

The deadline came quickly. Susan counted off the grey, cold days one by one until they were gone. She confirmed her reservation at a travel agency opposite the hotel, and on the afternoon of the day of her flight, she packed her bags.

Funny, she thought, how anonymous a hotel room seems when you arrive; and then you occupy it, you make it your own. Now the process was running in reverse. With her clothes folded into her suitcases, the closet empty and the key on the dresser—it was as if she had never moved in. Where had all the time gone? But that was one of those dumb, self-punishing questions.

Darkness came early these cloudy days. At four o'clock she flicked on the room lamps and began to dress for the flight. A seven-thirty flight, but Susan preferred to arrive early at airports. Dress and maybe catch a snack at the hotel coffee shop, then a cab to the airport. Check in by six or six-thirty . . . buy a book at the newsstand and camp out in a waiting room until the flight was ready to board.

She was standing in her slip when the phone rang.

She scolded herself for a sudden leap of hope. Reprieves did not come at the last minute. *Only in the movies, Susan.*

She picked up the receiver and said, "Yes?"

"Is that—" It was a woman's voice. "Is that Susan Christopher?"

Far away and unfamiliar, tremulous and odd. Susan frowned. "Who's this?"

"Amelie Desjardins. You remember me?"

Amelie who had lived with Benjamin. Amelie barefoot in the doorway of a slum apartment, radiating suspicion. "Of course." Susan wanted to add, *How did you get this number?* She asked instead, "Is anything wrong?"

"I have to talk to you."

"Well, I—the thing is—I have a plane to catch. I'm leaving tonight."

"Oh, shit. Oh! Well—listen—if you could just tell me, you know, where he *is*—just give me a number or something—just so I could *talk* to him—"

Susan said desperately, "I don't know!"

"*You* don't know? I thought that was why you came here—to take him away!"

"He left! John, I mean. He got scared and he just, uh, left." Should she be saying this? "What is it, Amelie, is there a problem?"

"It's my fucking brother! I think he wants to kill me."

Susan could not frame a response to this.

"I just thought if I could *talk* to somebody," Amelie said. Then she added, "But you mean it, don't you? You lost him, too."

"Yes. Well, I— If you could get here soon, maybe we could talk. I have some time before I absolutely need to leave. Is this connected with John?"

"Partly. Look, I don't want to make a problem for you—"

"No, no!—I mean, I *want* to talk."

"Well, if there's time—"

"Can you get here inside the hour?"

Pause. "Sure. It's not that far."

"I'll wait for you," Susan said.

———

They met in the lobby and then found a booth at the back of the coffee shop.

Amelie's eyes were puffy and bloodshot; her hair was down in matted bangs across her forehead. She wore jeans and a T-shirt under an oversized red plaid lumberjack shirt. Susan, sitting across from her, felt instantly helpless.

"It's Roch," Amelie said. "He's my brother."

The girl seemed anxious to talk; Susan listened carefully. She was not accustomed to having people come to her with their problems. It wasn't the sort of thing that happened to her. She paid close, somber attention as Amelie spoke.

Amelie had a brother named Roch who had followed her to Toronto from Montreal. "A real son-of-a-bitch. I mean, he has trouble dealing with people. I don't think he registers people at all, they just don't exist for him, unless they get in his way or humiliate him—and then his instinct is just to crush them, grind them under his foot. He can be pretty single-minded about it. I learned how to deal with it, you know, how to keep from making him mad. But it isn't always easy. When we came here—"

When they came to Toronto they had lived in the streets and Roch had encouraged Amelie into occasional prostitution.

"But that sounds like—I mean, you have to understand, it was the kind of thing a runaway kid might do. It happened maybe four or five times and it was a question of having money for food, a place to stay. It was a long time ago."

Susan nodded.

Eventually Amelie had found a job and a cheap apartment. Roch had taken a whole string of jobs, mostly lifting and carrying. He was strong, Amelie said, but he didn't get along with people. He'd been working for the last six months at the Bus Parcel Express depot down at Front Street, but he lost that when he put a choke-hold on his supervisor and almost killed him. Roch was outraged when they fired him. His life, Amelie seemed to imply, was a continuous series of these outrages: he would be provoked, he would respond, he would be punished for it. . . . "Christ knows what the guy said to him. Some kind of insult. So Roch practically breaks the man's neck, and he's fired, and it's business as usual, right? Except that, for Roch, every time this happens it's like brand-new. Like he's filing it away on some index card in his head: *fucked over again.*"

Amelie had avoided Roch fairly effectively for a few years. But the BPX firing had been a point-of-no-return . . . now Roch was back, and he had changed, Amelie said; he was closer to the edge than he had ever been before.

"Like this thing with Benjamin. Suddenly Roch is jealous. For three years he ignores me altogether, then suddenly he resents this guy I'm living with. What makes it worse is that Benjamin—or I guess it was John—did this humiliation thing on him, the fight they had. No real physical damage, but the *contempt*—you could feel it shooting out of him. And Roch just soaked it up. Charging his battery—you know what I mean? You could say Roch is at a very high voltage right now."

Amelie stopped long enough to finish the beer she'd ordered. Susan waited.

Amelie drained the glass. "Maybe it's better Benjamin left. I don't think he could stand up to Roch right now. I don't think— I'm not sure I can, either."

Susan said, "He's staying with you?"

"I can't make him leave."

"Is he hurting you?"

Amelie looked across the table, then reached up and pulled her hair away from her forehead. There was an angry blue bruise underneath.

Susan drew in her breath. "My God!"

Amelie shrugged. "I'm just worried he'll get worse."

"You should call the police!"

She laughed derisively. "Have you ever seen a domestic dispute call? I have. You know what happens? Fuck-all, is what happens. And it would make Roch really mad."

"You can leave, though, can't you?"

"It's my *apartment!*"

"I mean temporarily," Susan said. "There must be a women's shelter in the city. You could have a restraining order put on him—"

"A restraining order," Amelie said: the idea was comic. But she added, "Are there really shelters?"

"Well—we can find out. Let me make a couple of calls." Susan looked at her watch. "Oh, lord—my *plane!*"

"That's right," Amelie said. "You gotta go." She stood up; Susan fumbled out money for the check. Amelie added, "You expect to hear from him again?" Meaning John.

"I don't know," Susan admitted. "Maybe. Maybe you'll hear from him first. We have to keep in touch. Listen, there are phones in the lobby . . . let me make a couple of calls for you?"

Amelie shrugged.

Susan stopped at the front desk, hunting in her purse for the room key. Check out, locate a shelter in case Amelie needed it, then take a cab to the airport—there was still time for everything, but only just. She tapped the bell and the desk clerk hurried over. "Ms. Christopher—"

"Yes," she began. "I—"

"That call came through," the clerk said. "I suppose the one you've been waiting for? Long distance collect."

Susan just gaped.

"No message," the clerk said. "Except that he would try again in an hour or so."

Susan checked her watch a second time.

"When was this?"

"About twenty-five minutes ago."

"Thank you," Susan said. "I'll wait up in my room."

"Yes, ma'am. Was there anything else—?"

"No—not just now." She turned to Amelie. "You can wait with me if you like."

Amelie said, "Won't you miss your plane?"

"Yes," Susan said. "I will."

II

John said he would meet her Wednesday morning at the ferry docks at Tsawassen.

Dr. Kyriakides wired the money for her flight to B.C. and two tickets back. Susan helped Amelie check into a YWCA, spent a sleepless night at the hotel, then caught a taxi to the airport and a westbound plane.

It was windy and cold at the docks. Susan bought a cup of bitter coin-machine coffee and huddled in the waiting room. She was excited but terribly tired. She slept for a few minutes with her back against the wall, woke up stiff and uncomfortable—and saw John standing a few feet away.

He looked thin and worn, a duffel bag in one hand and a grey visor cap pulled down over his eyes. He was sun-brown and his hair was longer than she remembered. But it was John, not Benjamin . . . there was something in the way he stood . . . she knew at once.

She stood up. She had envisioned this moment, played it over in her mind a dozen times during the trip from Toronto. She wanted to embrace him but decided she didn't really know him well enough—it just seemed that way, after all the waiting.

She took his hands: a small, spontaneous gesture. "I'm glad you decided to call."

He looked at her for a long time. He reached up to touch her cheek, and the expression on his face . . . Susan could not take the measure of it; but there might have been surprise, curiosity, maybe even gratitude.

She said, "Can I ask what it was—why you changed your mind?"

He took his hand away and held it up in front of her.

His hand was trembling. It was a pronounced, involuntary tremor; Susan was suddenly afraid, watching it. He *was* sick—he was admitting it now.

He said, "I found out that I don't want to die."

———

She called Dr. Kyriakides from a booth in the airport, confirming the meeting. "He hasn't said it in so many words, but I think this is his way of telling us he needs us. That's important, isn't it?"

"Possibly," Dr. Kyriakides said. He sounds worried, Susan thought; or worse—he sounds frightened.

"Hey," she said, "the battle's over, isn't it? We're almost home."

"No," Dr. Kyriakides said. "I think you're mistaken. I think the battle has only just begun. I think we're a very long way from home."

PART II
CONTROLLED EXPERIMENTS

12

Maxim Kyriakides paid the taxi driver and watched as the automobile sped away, leaving him alone in the gravel driveway of the house north of Toronto in which he would be spending the next few months.

The house was a whitewashed pseudo-Georgian structure, isolated from its neighbors by groves of trees. Maxim had never seen it before. It belonged to a colleague, a University of Toronto professor named Collingwood, who was a member of what they had called "The Network" many years ago. The house was to have gone up for sale a week ago, but Collingwood had offered it to Maxim when Maxim explained the problem he was facing.

The house was suitably large. Maxim walked up the driveway to the big portico, fished a key from his pocket and inserted it into the lock on the double doors. Open, they admitted a wash of December sunlight into the tiled foyer. The house was cold; the heat had been turned off for some days.

But the electricity had been restored yesterday. Maxim flicked a switch and the lights winked on. The entrance hall yielded to a kitchen, a living room, a library. These were furnished, though sparsely—valuables had been removed and there were blank, pale spaces where paintings had been taken from the walls.

Well, he thought, that was appropriate, too. We shall all be entering a new, unfamiliar space. All three of us . . . all four, counting the French-Canadian girl Susan had mentioned. No, even more than that. Five, he thought, if you allowed Benjamin as a separate entity.

Maxim ascended the staircase carefully. He was healthy enough to pass for ten or fifteen years younger than his age. He was large but not fat; he had always walked for pleasure, sometimes great distances, and he supposed that habit had helped preserve his health. Still, he was conscious of his age. At sixty-eight, stairs were a chore to be undertaken with some seriousness. He remembered his Uncle Constantine moving through the house in Macedonia at this same solemn, considered pace. Constantine had been a schoolteacher and a cynical Communist, a friend of the rebel Veloukhiotis. Maxim was then a teenager and already an ideologue; he had read Marx with great determination. Now . . . is it possible, he wondered, that as children we're already learning how to be old? Had he been studying for infirmity under his uncle's slow tutelage?

The second floor of the house on the outskirts of Toronto exuded a closed-in, musty atmosphere. He wanted to open a window but dared not; that would only make it more difficult to heat these rooms when the furnace kicked on again. He stood by a bedroom window and gazed through its double panes across a wooded ravine. The ravine was stark and bare, a swath of perhaps a hundred yards between the house and a housing project crowded up against a major highway. The ravine afforded at least a little privacy, and that was good. The house, he thought, was as close to stateliness as one could achieve in such a prefabricated landscape.

He paused to scold himself for this momentary class snobbery, to which he was not even entitled. Maxim, though no longer a Communist like poor dead Constantine, had once considered himself a socialist; certainly he had never been wealthy.

But the important thing, he thought, is that I can work here.

It was John who had insisted on staying in Toronto. Maxim had wanted him to fly to Chicago with Susan. But John believed he would be safer on this side of the border—which might even be true, though Maxim had no evidence to suggest it—and certainly he would be more comfortable, less disoriented, in a familiar setting. So Maxim had arranged a sudden sabbatical, ostensibly for reasons of health (no one inquired too closely—one of the advantages of seniority and tenure), and borrowed this house from his friend.

Everything was in place except for the people, and they would be arriving tomorrow. Susan, this young woman Amelie . . . and John, whom Maxim had not set eyes upon for many years.

Resting a moment in the darkened hallway, he silently framed the forbidden words: *My son.*

Not literally, of course. Maxim had never married, never produced any children. Even his most intimate friends—possibly excepting those in the so-called Network—took him for an elderly bachelor of the generic sort, married to his research and his teaching. And that was, in fact, largely true. But no one's life is as simple as his friends believe.

In a real sense, Maxim thought, I created John. What else is fatherhood? This was, if anything, even more profound. A virgin fatherhood.

He thought, *I could have raised him.*

It was one of those thoughts that came to him periodically, unbidden and unwelcome. Ordinarily, he would have shunted it aside. It was not useful. But now, with the prospect of facing John once again, there was no avoiding it.

If they hadn't taken him away—

If I hadn't allowed *them to take him away—*

But, no. He was too old to regret his life. You do what you do. And then you do what you can.

He sat down in a chair in the entranceway to wait for the deliveries he had been told to expect: a few pharmaceuticals, a tape recorder, his notebooks. Bundled in a huge coat and away from the wind, he was warm enough—except for his feet. Warm enough, anyway, to drift toward sleep.

Drifting, he was briefly assailed by a dream-image of John standing before him, John grown unnaturally tall, pointing a finger of accusation and pronouncing the word "Liar!" The vision was disturbing and it startled him awake; he sat up blinking.

The afternoon light had dimmed. The house was dark.

He rubbed his face, sighing. Traitorous sleep. But he supposed there was some truth in his dream. He had implied to Susan that there was some treatment available for John; presumably she had passed this implication on. Poor trusting Susan, who believed in his miraculous powers. In fact there was nothing for John in this house but a warm bed in which to endure his crisis. And my notebook, Maxim thought. My obdurate curiosity, and my guilt.

Tests would be run, of course, and there was dopamine, which had relieved some symptoms in the animal studies. But there was nothing to forestall the ultimate resolution. Unwillingly, Maxim recalled his laboratory chimps, the animals prostrate and comatose or consumed by fever. In the initial tests—before John was born —the beasts had not been allowed to live long enough to exhibit symptoms; they were grotesques, capable of understanding a few words of written English and copying the alphabet from children's books; they were destroyed as a potential embarrassment. But Dr. Kyriakides had allowed his second animals, his private experiment, to live to maturity—caged homunculi with enlarged skulls and wizened, cynical faces. He had watched them live out their truncated lives, scratching *apple* and *orange* onto yellow copypaper or probing their fur with the pencils, and dropping into recurrent fevers which he mistook at first for some form of malaria; then battering themselves against their cages and screeching, as if they had suffered some unendurable insight into their own condition—collapsing at last into a febrile unconsciousness.

Most died. Some recovered, but never fully. Never regained their facility with the pencil, never remembered how to operate the infant toys. The ones who survived lived on as lab animals, caged and listless . . . though an x-ray or an autopsy might reveal certain unusual cerebral lesions. Whatever its outcome, the affliction was universal.

And now John.

I didn't mean this to happen.

But it had happened anyway.

Maxim stood up, groaning. Old bones. But his feet were not as cold as they had been, and he realized that the gas must have been turned on while he slept; the house had begun to warm around him.

13

Roch said he was going out for the day—looking for work, he said. Amelie watched from the kitchen window as he drove off in his battered green Chevy van. Then she telephoned Susan.

"Today," she said. "Can you pick me up?"

"All right," Susan said.

Amelie hurried to pack her things.

Not that there was much to pack. A suitcase full of clothes; the stereo, the TV set. None of the furniture was worth hanging on to; if there had been time she would have sent it back to the Salvation Army depot where she'd found it. But the arrangements had to be made in secret, and quickly, so that Roch wouldn't find out. He had been in a tolerable mood through Christmas and Amelie didn't want to provoke anything before she left. Above all, she didn't want him to find out where she was going.

Susan had said she would come by with the car around noon. At eleven forty-five Amelie hiked her belongings out to the curb where they sat in a small, unimpressive heap. She wrapped herself in a jacket and stood shivering next to the luggage. It was a cold January day and the clouds had begun to wring out a few flakes of snow. The sidewalk was clear but cold; ice stood in pockets in the grassy verge. It was at least not one of those hideously cold days you sometimes get in January and February, when the air steals your breath and even the short walk to the bus stop is an endurance test—but it felt like those days were coming. Amelie decided she would need a new winter coat, not just this jacket. She used to own a parka (from the Thrift Village over on Augusta), but she'd thrown it away when the seams ripped under the arms.

She looked up and down the street anxiously, but there was no sign of Susan's car.

It felt funny, leaving the apartment behind . . . leaving it to Roch, who would probably have to be evicted. But she'd left so much behind already. Her job at the restaurant, for instance. Susan claimed that Dr. Kyriakides would be able to find her another job soon, and maybe that was true or maybe not; but she couldn't stay on at the Goodtime, because Roch would be sure to find her there. She had no illusions about Roch. She had lived with her brother for most of the past month and she understood that whatever was wrong with him—she thought of it as a kind of broken wheel inside him—was getting worse. The wheel was running loose; it had come free of all the gears and governors and pretty soon it might wreck the machine entirely. You could tell by the noise, by the smell of hot metal and simmering oil.

Amelie, who smoked cigarettes very occasionally, fished one out of her purse now and lit it. It made her feel warmer. But then she coughed and felt mildly guilty—felt the pressure of all those Public Health ads on TV. She took a last drag and butted out the cigarette against the icy ground. Her watch said 11:58. She whispered, "Come on, Susan!" Her breath made clouds in the cold air.

She tried to remember what Susan Christopher was driving these days. She had seen the car a couple of times: a rented

Honda, she recalled, some drab color—beige or brown? Kind of box-shaped. Maybe that was it, at the corner?

But no, the distant grey automobile rolled on without turning. There was a stillness in the air, the eerie calm of a cold weekday noon. Everybody was inside having lunch. Amelie thought randomly of the École in Montreal, bag lunches in the dingy cafeteria and pale winter light through the mullioned windows. Dead hours like this. Behind closed eyes she pictured the Honda, willing it to arrive. Susan, goddamn! This was *dangerous*.

She opened her eyes then and looked down the street. A vehicle turned the corner. But it was not Susan's Honda.

It was Roch's green van.

She stood up, panicked. But what was there to do? Hide in the apartment? How was she supposed to *explain* this—the little Sony TV, the stereo, taped Tourister luggage, all sitting at the curb in a neat pile? She wanted to run but couldn't make her feet move. Susan will come, she thought, and I'll jump into the car and we'll zoom away. . . .

But Susan didn't come. The van rolled to a stop beside her.

Oh, Amelie thought, oh, *shit!*

Roch cracked open the door on the passenger side. She saw him peering out from the dimness inside, and the expression on his face was stony and opaque. He said, "Going somewhere?"

It was like being back in school. Latin class, she thought dizzily. Inevitably, the Sister would ask her to decline some verb. And Amelie, who could not get a grip on Latin, would stand beside her desk in mute humiliation. This same wordlessness overtook her now. She could not run. She could not speak.

Roch said disgustedly, "Get in."

Meekly, Amelie obeyed.

––––––––

Susan turned the corner and saw Amelie's possessions piled on the curb . . . then registered the green van idling ahead. It was Roch's van. Susan had seen it parked at the building before; Amelie had pointed it out. *No,* she thought—and pulled the Honda over before she could be spotted.

She watched Amelie climb into the van.

Susan's mind was racing. She wished John was here, or Dr. Kyriakides. She remembered the bruise Amelie had showed her . . . remembered Amelie's description of Roch.

She was what, five minutes late? She shouldn't have stopped for coffee at the hotel. Shouldn't have come up Yonge Street; the traffic was bad. Shouldn't have—

But that was stupid. Not helpful at all.

She watched the green van roll away. It turned right at the next corner.

Now or never, Susan thought.

She gunned the Honda down the street.

————

Pretty soon, Amelie understood where Roch was taking her.

When she was young and on the street in Toronto she had heard about Cherry Beach. It was a bleak strip of shoreline east of the harbor, and if a cop picked you up after midnight, for vagrancy, say, or trespassing, or prostitution, and if you said the wrong thing, then the cop might drive you out to Cherry Beach and do some work on your attitude. It was called Cherry Beach Express, and although Amelie had never experienced it she knew people who had. She was always afraid it was Roch who would end up out there—permanently damaged, maybe, because he did not know when to shut up and lie down.

Now Roch was driving her past the peeling towers of grain silos and the shadows of lake freighters, down industrial alleys and across rusted railway sidings. Cherry Beach Express. Because Roch understood how punishment worked. Obviously it was punishment he had on his mind right now.

But it's daylight, she thought, someone will see us—

But that was stupid. She knew better.

She looked at Roch, a careful sideways glance. His lips were compressed and pale. He was nodding to himself, as if he had expected this all along, ratty old Amelie showing her true colors at last. This was not even hatred, Amelie thought; it was something much colder and vaster than that.

She said, "Roch, I—"

"Don't talk," he said. "Shut up."

She bit her lip.

The van rolled to a stop far along the isolated shoreline, obscured from the road by a stand of leafless maples. Roch reached across and opened Amelie's door, then pushed her out. She stumbled onto the cold, compacted sand. The air was brittle with moisture and she could hear the waves lapping at the shore. Far off, somewhere in the harbor, a freighter sounded its horn.

Roch climbed down after her. Amelie fought the urge to run. There was nowhere to go; Roch was fast and she would only make him mad. She stood with her hands at her side, breathing hard.

Roch stood in front of her, close enough for her to smell his breath.

He said, "You don't trust me."

She said, "That's not true!"

He slapped her. It was a hard, stinging, open-handed slap; it rocked her head to the right. Roch was strong . . . he still worked out in the gym twice a week. Amelie knew this, because he had borrowed money from her to keep his membership current.

"You don't trust me," he said, "and you're lying to me. What kind of thing is that to do? Christ, I'm your brother! Doesn't that mean anything to you?"

He expected an answer. Amelie was rigid, frightened. "Sure it means something to me."

"Liar," Roch said sadly.

"No, I mean it! I mean—Jesus Christ, Roch!"

He grabbed her wrists; his grip was powerful. "You were running away."

Amelie could not hold his gaze. She looked at the lake, instead, grey under grey clouds.

"Running away from home," Roch elaborated. "Look at me, goddammit!"

He took her jaw in his right hand and forced her to face him. His hand traveled up along her cheek in a gesture that was almost a caress; then he took a handful of her hair and twisted it. Amelie said, "Ow!" and began to cry.

"You were going somewhere," he said.

"I was moving out," she said. "All right? I'm sick of that place!"

"You didn't tell me," Roch said patiently. "You could have told me."

"I thought you'd get mad!"

He seemed puzzled. "Why? Why would I get mad? I mean, maybe you're right. We need a bigger place. Hey, I'm reasonable." His grip tightened on her hair. "But that's not all of it— right?"

"Shit," Amelie said.

"Don't use bad language," Roch said. "It makes you sound cheap." He was thinking; his face was contorted with the effort of it. "You wanted to get rid of me. That's it, isn't it? Or else—it's that guy you shacked up with, right? He's back—right?"

Amelie hated it when Roch talked about Benjamin. Dirty, dangerous words. "Shut up," she said.

He slapped her again. This time, with his left hand firmly tangled in her hair, it was worse.

"Don't talk to me like that," he said.

She moaned.

"He's back—right?"

After a long pause, Amelie nodded.

"You were going to stay with him."

Pause, nod again. Snow was falling gently now. She felt the flakes against her burning cheek.

"Well, you can go," Roch said. Amelie looked up. Roch smiled. "You can go if you want to. Sure! Go with him! I'm on your side! All I want—I just want you to prove you trust me. I just want you to tell me where I can find you."

"No," Amelie said instantly.

"No? You won't tell me?"

"I—I don't know, Roch, we haven't—"

But she did know. Susan had given her the address of the house; Amelie had written it down and hidden it in her purse. Roch understood this, of course. He always knew when she was lying.

This time, though, he didn't slap her. This time he jerked his knee up into her belly and at the same time released her hair, put his hand in a frightening grip around her face and pushed. Amelie fell to the ground, doubled over and gasping for breath. The pain was enormous.

Roch said, in a tone of weary patience, "All you have to do is tell me."

Amelie blinked. She felt like throwing up. She rose to her knees, and then—past Roch, a great distance back the way they'd come along the shore road—she saw a flicker of light. It was a reflection from a car window, and the car was rolling along in slow motion, and it was grey—a grey Honda.

It was Susan, Amelie realized, who must have followed them from the rooming house.

She looked up at Roch, trying hard to disguise her emotion.

He took her hair and dragged her up. Amelie grabbed a double handful of cold, gritty beach sand . . . and then she was on her feet.

She had seen this in movies. You took a handful of dirt—

Roch frowned. "What now?" Reading her face.

Amelie brought both hands up and thrust them forward, spraying the beach sand into Roch's eyes.

"What the *fuck*—!" he screamed.

Amelie ducked past his groping hands toward the Honda. She saw Susan accelerate suddenly down the gritty tarmac. *Hurry, Susan!*

But the sand-in-the-eyes thing was not as paralyzing as it looked on TV. Roch turned and scrambled after her. She could hear the thump of his big feet against the beach. The sandy beach slowed her down; it was like running in a dream . . . but maybe it would slow Roch down, too. Amelie saw the Honda speeding toward her as Susan realized what had happened. Amelie drew in great ragged gasps of frigid air.

The Honda veered away from the road and ran a few yards along the verge. It wavered, and Amelie saw Susan groping across the passenger seat to unlock the far door. The door swung open as the Honda curved back to the road. Amelie focused all her attention on that door. It was her only way out of here. Because Roch was mad enough now that he might kill her . . . maybe not on purpose; but he was strong; she was not.

He was right behind her now. She could hear his angry breathing. She didn't look back, because surely that would be the end; because he might be *right there* with his arms outstretched; she might freeze in her tracks, seeing him. She watched the Honda roll forward in lazy dream-time and thought, *Here I am, okay, right here, Susan!*

Then she felt a tug as Roch closed his hand on her jacket. She pulled away, but only briefly. She stumbled, and Roch tackled her —a football tackle; she went down winded and breathless.

When she opened her eyes he was kneeling over her. But the look on his face was not triumphant; it was queerly mechanical, a vacant gaze that was focused on her only approximately. But his fist was raised and it was obvious what he meant to do. Amelie tried to squirm away but his other hand was clamped in a fierce grip around her neck.

Amelie twisted her head to one side in time to see the front tires of the Honda spitting sand as the car braked beside her.

Susan! Amelie thought. But it wasn't Susan who saved her, really; it was the passenger-side door, which flew open as the Honda stopped and caught Roch across the head and shoulders. Roch slumped forward and his weight was immense, but the grip around her neck had loosened and Amelie slid out from under the limp bulk of her brother.

Susan pulled her inside the car. Amelie slammed the door and hammered down the lock. Susan stepped down on the accelerator. The little car revved against the sand for a long, heartstopping moment; then the rear wheels seemed to bite down and the Honda shot forward. The car missed a leafless maple by inches . . . Amelie cringed . . . then they were back on solid tarmac and rocketing down the lakeshore road.

Amelie knelt on the vinyl carseat and peered through the rear window. She saw Roch stand up. He shook himself—she thought of a wet dog shaking itself dry—then stumbled toward his van.

"He's coming after us," she said.

Susan said, "Relax," though she was breathing hard. The Honda turned left and roared through the industrial wasteland. Amelie watched vigilantly but saw no sign of Roch. Then they were into traffic and there was no chance of him following; Amelie sighed and slumped down in the seat.

"Thanks," she said.

"It's okay," Susan said.

————

Amelie stared vacantly through the window. The snow was falling harder now. The afternoon was turning dark.

"Are you all right?" Susan asked.

Amelie touched the sore part of her cheek. It would swell and bruise; it would look shitty. She was bruised down around her belly, too. But it was nothing terrible. She told Susan so.

"Nice guy," Susan commented.

Amelie shrugged.

"I guess he wanted to know where you were going?"

"Yes," Amelie said.

"Did you tell him?"

"No."

"That's why he hit you."

Amelie nodded.

Susan said, "That was pretty brave—not telling him."

"Brave?" Amelie said. She almost laughed. "Jesus, Susan!—for a smart person, you're not very bright sometimes."

———

They took a long route back to make sure Roch hadn't managed to follow. Coming up on Amelie's rooming house, Susan slowed. There was no sign of the van. . . . Roch wasn't here.

But he had been. He must not have tried to follow at all; he must have come straight back. Amelie's things had been trashed. "Oh, no," Susan said. She waited for some response from Amelie, but there was none. Amelie only looked morosely at the pile of wreckage that had been her stereo, the little TV, a suitcase full of clothes. "Stop," she said, as the Honda rolled past. She opened the passenger door and leaned out to collect a couple of blouses, some tapes, a pair of Levis from the snowy gutter. She held these on her lap.

"All that other stuff," Susan said, "you know, we can replace all that."

Amelie shrugged and closed the door. She did not look back as Susan drove away.

———

Amelie was silent during most of the ride to the house Dr. Kyriakides had rented, seeming to watch the snow that had begun to accumulate across the brown farm fields and the cold marshes north of the city. Susan drove carefully, grateful for the silence and the chance to begin to assimilate everything that had happened. That terrible man . . . and, my God, she had almost killed him, slamming the car door into him . . . !

"The thing is," Amelie said quietly, "I just don't know."

Susan looked across at her. "Know what?"

Amelie studied her fingernails.

"About Roch," she said. "I don't know whether we can do something like that to him. I mean, and get away with it." She turned her large, shiny eyes on Susan. "I don't know if he'll let us."

14

From the notebooks of Maxim Kyriakides:

Finally we are all together in this house, presumably for the duration of the winter. (The snow continues to deepen; we are all confined by it—though of course it isn't the snow that keeps us together.) In our isolation, certain things have become clear.

I begin to realize that there is, underlying all else, the question of Benjamin. The question of his sudden new presence in John's life. The question of where Benjamin comes from, and perhaps what he will become.

———

From the taped transcripts of their meetings: Maxim Kyriakides and John Shaw, January 12:

Kyriakides: Hello, John. Please, sit down. [The sound of a chair being pulled up.] This is the room I've set aside for my work. I hope we'll be meeting here often. [A long pause.] You're staring at me. . . . Is something wrong?

John: [His voice firm but somewhat subdued.] I'm wondering what you want from me.

Kyriakides: Well, that's a complicated question. I won't attempt to lie to you. Let's say—for the moment, I'm your doctor.

John: You won't lie, but you will condescend to me.

Kyriakides: Is that what I'm doing?

John: I know you, Max. It's been years, obviously. But I haven't forgotten.

Kyriakides: You understand, this is difficult for me, too. *I* know *you*. I know what you're capable of. I know what you could do as a child. . . . I can guess what you're capable of now. So there's an element of caution.

John: Of fear.

Kyriakides: If you like. Does that make you happy?

John: Is this psychoanalysis?

Kyriakides: I suppose, on one level, it is. I can be a better judge of what's happening if we're able to talk to one another.

John: You can judge my deterioration, you mean.

Kyriakides: If it happens that way. I hope to be able to prevent it. [A pause.] We're being honest, here.

John: All those years . . .

Kyriakides: You resented me.

John: No, Max. I hated you.

———

John: Tell me about the treatment.

Kyriakides: Treatment can't begin until we have more information. I have an arrangement with Dr. Collingwood—he's a neurologist. He'll be examining you, and he has connections at the University and at Toronto General, so we'll have access to PET scanners and that sort of thing. We need a complete neurological workup before we can proceed.

John: In other words, you don't have any treatment in mind.

Kyriakides: What I mean is that I won't discuss treatment until we know more. I don't want you second-guessing me.

John: Even if my guesses are better than yours.

Kyriakides: It isn't a question of pride. I admit that I need a certain amount of elbow-room—emotional, intellectual.

John: You did animal studies.

Kyriakides: Yes . . .

John: The animals experienced loss of cortical tissue.

Kyriakides: They did.

John: Did they die? [Pause.] Max? Did the animals die?

Kyriakides: Some of them—yes.

———

Kyriakides: I think we have to begin by talking about Benjamin.

John: I won't submit to amateur psychoanalysis—I thought I'd made that clear. The problem is physiological.

Kyriakides: The symptoms may not be. This is relevant, John. You do accept the implication that Benjamin—his manifestation over the last year or two—is a symptom?

John: Of something. Are you asking me to diagnose myself?

Kyriakides: I'm trying to justify my interest.

John: You're suggesting Benjamin began to manifest as a result of cortical disfunction. Maybe so, maybe not. Sometimes I think I just . . . lost interest. When I invented him, you know, it was a willful act—I wanted someone to run all the routine chores, to gratify all the expectations I couldn't fulfill. He was a kind of autopilot. Do you understand? But I think that's the danger. I created an autonomous cortical subroutine and allowed it access to my voluntary motor activity. That must have created profound neural channeling—it's not the sort of thing you can simply erase. And when being John Shaw became too difficult, Benjamin was there. He was waiting.

Kyriakides: Why was it difficult to be John Shaw?

John: Maybe I was sick. Maybe I was just . . . tired.

Kyriakides: But it was a conscious decision.

John: To resurrect Benjamin? No—it was not.

Kyriakides: Therefore we have to examine it.

John: This is still parlor Freudianism, Max. Benjamin as the unconscious mind of John Shaw. *The Three Faces of Eve.* But it isn't like that. You should know better. Freud was a bourgeois apologist, wasn't he?

Kyriakides: I'm not a Marxist anymore, John.

John: How they fade—the passions of our youth.

Kyriakides: You're trying to nettle me. Is that why you keep calling me "Max"?

John: That's what *they* used to call you, isn't it? Your colleagues in the Network?

Kyriakides: You know about that?

John: I overheard things—even as a child. I'm sorry if it bothers you, calling you Max. I would feel a little odd about using formal titles, I'm afraid.

Kyriakides: Your conscious mind is exceptional, John. I haven't made the mistake of assuming your unconscious mind is any less prodigious. Nor should you.

John: Superman and superego.

Kyriakides: Obviously I can't force you to talk about Benjamin. But the implication is that you find the topic disturbing.

John: I'm about to be evicted from my body, Max. Or lose my mind. Of course it's disturbing.

Kyriakides: Yes, but there may be another way to think about it. I wonder if Benjamin isn't a kind of survival instinct? Unconscious—I'm forced to use the word. But profound. Maybe you've resurrected him for a reason. He's your creation, after all. He may be the key to your survival.

John: A rapprochement. We learn to love each other. It's a cliché.

Kyriakides: Something more subtle than that. What if, neurologically speaking, Benjamin is a sort of life-raft? The scrap of wood that survives the disaster?

John: Then I should cling to him?

Kyriakides: You should *become* him. You should *colonize* him.

John: You can't put all your cargo on a raft, Max. It sinks.

Kyriakides: No . . . but perhaps you can save what's most valuable.

John: I'm tired—I'd like to go back to my room.

Kyriakides: I won't keep you. Only one more question. You've been remarkably successful at restraining Benjamin ever since Susan contacted you—

John: That's *why* I'm tired, Max.

Kyriakides: Do you expect him to manifest his presence soon?

John: It wouldn't surprise me. I'm not sure how to keep him away. In Indonesia, they chase away evil spirits by banging pots and pans. Would that work, Max? Stimulants are also good. But I don't suppose Dr. Collingwood would be willing to write a prescription. [A pause.] You want to meet him—is that it?

Kyriakides: Is that difficult to understand?

John: You think he can help you?

Kyriakides: Susan says he's been helpful.

John: Cooperating in his own annihilation?

Kyriakides: If that's what it means. It may not. Do you despise him so much? You created him, after all. He's a part of you.

John: I don't think even Shakespeare would enjoy having Hamlet compete for the control of his body—do you, Max?

Kyriakides: Hamlet was imaginary—

John: So was Benjamin.

Kyriakides: But he isn't any longer. Surely that's the point? You've created a living human being. You have to live with the consequences.

John: I yield to your experience in the matter.

From the notebooks of Maxim Kyriakides:

We live together in mutual isolation. The house is big enough that we are not forced into interaction; therefore that interaction has not yet begun. Susan and Amelie are nervous with each other—

rivals, in a sense, though I don't think either of them quite realize that. I wonder about the wisdom of taking in Amelie, but Susan was insistent; and she may be useful in dealing with Benjamin . . . when Benjamin finally appears.

He is the ghost that hovers over this house. I do not know him. I do not know what role he has to play, or whether he will be willing to play it. Tomorrow John enters the hospital for tests; perhaps after that we will have some useful approach to the problem—certainly we will all feel less aimless.

In the meantime I am chafing under John's hostility. It is under-standable and perhaps even therapeutic for him. Nevertheless it hurts. I am in every important sense his father. He must know I feel that way—it was always impossible to hide intense emotion from him. But he resents it, or uses it against me.

And I cannot blame him.

My God, that is the worst of it.

He believes I abandoned him.

He's right.

15

Susan drove everyone into the city in her Honda—she thought of it as hers, though it was Dr. Kyriakides who had taken out the lease. Dr. Kyriakides didn't drive; the task had fallen to Susan by default; therefore, it was her car.

It was a cold, clear January day, the sun bright but barely strong enough to warm the tarmac. Snowplows had left huge hills of snow on each side of the highway. It had been a snowy winter and the indications were that it would get worse. No snow today but lots of icy runoff; Susan was cautious on turns; downtown, she parked in an underground lot.

Today was the day John was scheduled for tests at Toronto General. TGH was the city's central hospital, and as she passed through the lobby Susan was reminded of every other hospital she had ever seen. The corridors were pastel green and blue, the paint abraded where gurney carts had bumped against the walls; mysterious doors opened into mysterious rooms; doctors and interns bustled past with fixed, distant expressions. Dr. Kyriakides introduced John to another doctor, a man named Collingwood, while Susan and Amelie staked out chairs in a waiting room. Collingwood was grey-haired, bearded, stout. He spoke in a subdued tone, then led John away down the corridor. Dr. Kyriakides sighed, and rooted out a copy of *Newsweek* from the sidetable. Amelie had found *People*. Susan could not concentrate on reading; she kept her eyes on the corridor beyond the waiting-room door.

She glimpsed John when he passed a second time, without stopping, as he followed Dr. Collingwood down the hall. He had changed into a green hospital gown and paper slippers, and the effect, Susan thought, was of an immense indignity.

When Susan was fourteen years old she had decided to become a doctor. It was a serious ambition, but in the end she realized she didn't have the stomach for it. Undergraduate biology courses offered confirming evidence that her squeamishness was fundamental, inarguable, and permanent. That was when she detoured into cellular biology. She could deal with living systems as whole entities or as specimens on a slide; it was only that queasy middle ground, the surgeon's world of pumping blood and palpitating organs, that repelled her. That was the world where her father's cancer had lived. Of all the ugly facets of his death she resented this perhaps most of all, that he had become an ecology for a virulent and alien growth. It struck her now that what she missed most was the illusion of his sturdiness. Fathers should be solid, front to back, Susan thought. Otherwise nothing was certain. Anything could happen.

Maybe that was how John felt about Dr. Kyriakides.

But, disappointingly, she hadn't been able to talk to John much in the few days he had been back from Vancouver. He was moody; he had isolated himself in his room. Susan had passed his door and seen him pecking at a computer terminal, curious (but vaguely familiar) symbols flowing across the monitor. She wanted to go in, talk to him, say something that would make him happy. But it was not a privilege she had earned. No real intimacy had passed between them and Susan felt ashamed of her feelings, the schoolgirl crush she had obviously developed. John was, as Dr. Kyriakides continued to insist, in some sense not even truly human.

But Susan knew what it was like to feel set apart, to feel different. Growing up in a California suburb, bookish and shy, citizen of an invisible country somewhere between Fantasyland and Pasadena, she would have welcomed the idea of a gentle superhuman sweeping her off her feet.

Except that he did not sweep. And "superhuman" didn't mean what it should. And he was not even especially gentle.

And worse—unless Dr. Kyriakides could do something about it —he might be dying, or at the very least losing himself . . . *leaving me,* Susan thought childishly; voyaging off, like her father, wherever people go when they leave their sullen, grieving families abandoned by the graveside.

————

But these were hospital thoughts. Susan walked down the corridor to a vending-machine cafeteria and bought herself a cup of coffee, hoping to shake the mood. Machine coffee in a styrofoam cup, cloyingly sweet and hot enough to raise blisters. She liked it.

When she got back to the waiting room Dr. Collingwood was there. He was a bear-shaped man, but not really large; he was only just as tall as Susan and the effect, as he turned to face her, was of some stern but basically amiable big animal. "This is Susan?" he asked.

Dr. Kyriakides nodded.

Collingwood said, "We have John in a room upstairs while we wait for time on the scanner. He asked for you to come up."

Susan was a little flattered, a little frightened. She followed Collingwood to the elevators and up two floors, then down an identical corridor to a small room in which John was sitting in his hospital gown.

Collingwood closed the door and left them alone.

John motioned to a chair. Susan sat with her hands primly in her lap.

He said, "You look more nervous than I am."

"*Are* you nervous?"

"Not about the PET scan. Apprehensive about the results, obviously. Hospitals frighten you?"

"Yes." She didn't explain why.

He said, "I brought this."

He reached into a day bag beside his chair and lifted out a portable chess set in a folding wooden box. "We have some time to kill while they warm up the machinery. If you don't mind, I thought I'd like a game."

She smiled. "You'll win."

"But that's not why I play." He sounded almost sheepish. "I like the patterns. It's like a dance. I like to watch it unfold. Is it all right?"

"Of course," Susan said.

He cleared away a stack of magazines from the courtesy table and set up the game. Susan opened with her king's pawn; John replied in kind. It was a gentle opening, a Giuco Piano, the so-called Quiet Game.

She studied the board. He said, "You think I've been avoiding you."

She was startled out of her thoughts. "Well, I—"

"Because I have been. Not avoiding you personally. It's just that I didn't want to face the questions."

She could only echo, "Questions?"

"The questions you never asked because you were afraid of what I might say. Questions about what I am. About what it's like, being what I am."

Susan felt herself blushing. *What kind of monster are you?*—it was true; the question had never been far away, had it?

She moved a knight, mainly to conceal her nervousness.

"I thought we should talk about it now," John said. "If you want to."

"I've thought about it," she admitted. "I've tried to imagine it."

"Did Max ever talk about me—about his work, in any detail?"

"I was never even allowed to see his lab animals. Nothing beyond the cellular level. Not much theory."

"Part of the problem is that we don't have an adequate vocabulary. People talk about 'intelligence' as if it consisted of certain discrete acts—solving problems, acquiring knowledge and storing it. Most of the standard tests reflect that. But it's really a superstition. When you talk about intelligence what you're dealing with is human consciousness, which is not simple or schematic. I think even Max knows better now."

He advanced his queen's knight pawn. Susan gazed at the board abstractly; she couldn't concentrate on the game.

He said, "There's an evolutionary question about intelligence, what it's for and how it arose. There's a theory that intelligence evolved along with the upright posture, and for a similar reason. Among other things, Susan, a neuron is a clock—a timing device. But a single neuron has a widely variable firing time—it's a clock but not a very good one." He brought out his king's knight. "Two neurons are a little better, because the errors begin to average out. Three neurons are better still, and so on. And clocks are good for operations involving timing. For instance, a dog: a dog is fairly good at catching things. But a dog couldn't throw a rock at a moving target even if the dog were anatomically equipped to do so. Taking aim at a moving target makes demands on the neural clock the dog just can't meet. Even the primates: you can't train an ape to throw a baseball with any accuracy. Making an accurate baseball pitch means solving a complex differential equation, and doing it on the molecular level. It takes neurons."

Susan marched her king's bishop down the ranks.

"If the theory is correct," John said, "then we evolved all this neocortical tissue so that we could stand on our hind legs and throw stones. Consciousness—intelligence—was the unforeseen side effect. Because the very calculation, the act of estimating speed and distance, of picking up the stone and taking aim, it *exiles you from time.* You understand, Susan? 'If the antelope is *there,* and I aim over *there'*—it implies I and thou, self and other, birth and mortality. Makes you human. Not just *I am* but *I was* and *I will be.* Fruit of the tree of knowledge. It makes you the animal that stands just a little bit outside of time."

His own bishop came rolling out. It was as if his hands were playing chess for him while he spoke. Susan responded with a reflexive pawn move, awed by this outrush of words.

"When Max was doing his work, of course, no one thought of intelligence this way. It was all much more linear: brains were calculating machines and we had better calculators than the apes. And there was no theoretical cap on it—you might imagine building a better brain the way the cybernetics people were upgrading Univac. Building a better human being. I think what Max imagined was a kind of ultimate Socialist Man, rational and benevolent." John advanced his queen's pawn a square, smiling to himself. "It didn't occur to him that he might be creating the more perfect baseball player. Or that a man with more cortical tissue might have more terrifying dreams. Or that 'intelligence' is a kind of exile from temporal experience—that he might be engineering a creature more wholly alienated than anything that had walked the earth before. Lost in time. Your queen's pawn."

"What?" Susan was startled.

"You're thinking of moving your queen's pawn. Not a bad move, actually."

"It's that obvious?"

"There are only so many reasonable moves available—and you're a reasonable player. But cautious, sometimes timid. That rules out a few things. Also, it's not hard to tell what part of the board you're focused on. And there are clues when you're about to move. You lean forward a little. You clench your right hand. Yes, it's that obvious."

"I don't like the idea of being so—transparent."

"No one does."

She hesitated, then pushed the pawn anyway. He continued, "This is by way of a warning."

"I'm sorry?"

"You see, I know why you're here. Here in this room, here with me. You're here because you have the unusual perversion of falling in love with amiable monsters. And that's what you mistook me for."

This is the kind of monster I am, he was saying: a genuine one, and not amiable at all.

She should have answered with something polite and distancing (to reassure him); or she should have stood up and walked out (because he was right). She did neither. She was feeling reckless and disoriented; she obeyed a momentary impulse and stared back at him. "What about you? You don't feel anything? You're so g-goddamn *aloof?* That's why you told me your life story that day in Kensington Market? That's why you came back from your island?" She clenched her fists under the table. "Tell the truth: do you at least l-*like* me?"

He blinked—it wasn't the question he had been expecting. Maybe, she thought, that was a good sign.

The room was silent for a moment; she could hear the ventilators humming.

"I could lie," John said slowly. "How would you know?"

"I wouldn't. I would trust you."

"I've lied to other people. Cheated other people. Stolen from them." He looked away. "Once I made love to a woman and left the bed wondering whether I'd committed an act of bestiality. That's a stunningly arrogant question to ask yourself. The terrible thing is, I don't know the answer."

"Then answer *my* question."

He looked back at the board. "Yes," he said quietly. "I like you." Regarded her calmly. "You're thinking of moving your queen's bishop."

Damn his infuriating confidence! "No," she said, "I'm *not.*"

"No?"

Obeying another impulse: "My knight. There—see? If I move him back into the first rank I uncover the rook's threat on your queen. While you're getting her out of harm's way, the knight takes the black bishop." She lifted the knight and thumped it down defiantly.

John stared at the board. *Surprised him again,* Susan thought. Finally he advanced his queen, developing a threat toward her rook . . . but the rook was defended; his bishop was not. She took the piece.

Seven moves later he had cut through her pawn ranks and opened the white king to attack. But his own defenses were a shambles; his castled king was locked in by her rooks. She was coordinating a strong final assault when he advanced his queen through an opening she had not noticed. "Mate," he said breathlessly.

But he was sweating. He looked up at her, and the look on his face now was the expression of a frightened child.

Susan understood suddenly what this tepid victory implied.

"Oh," she said. She reached for his hand across the table; it was feverishly warm. "John—"

But then the door opened: Dr. Collingwood, with Dr. Kyriakides behind him.

Collingwood cleared his throat. "We're ready now."

———

Maxim Kyriakides watched through a glass dividing wall as a nurse installed John in the bone-white ring of the PET scanner and administered an injection of glucose laced with fluorine-18, a radioactive isotope. The isotope would diffuse through the tissues of his body, breaking down and releasing tiny bursts of radioactivity.

The video monitor, over which Collingwood was hovering like a protective parent, would then translate this radiation into a picture of John's brain. Rather, Maxim thought, of the *activity* of his brain, not specifically the physical structure; this was the superiority of the PET scanner over a CAT. Maxim had never operated such a device; he was more strictly a creature of the test tube, the laboratory animal, the microscope. Consequently he watched from a respectful distance as the images began to scroll up.

"Interesting," Collingwood said.

"Butterflies," Kyriakides said quietly.

"Hm?"

"Or Rorschach tests. Like the ones they gave us as undergraduates. Ink blots. Except these are red and blue."

In fact they were images of John's functioning brain, and Maxim was able to recognize the left and right occipitals, the temporal lobes, as the scanner read its sequential slices through the skull. But the vivid colors meant nothing to him.

Res extensa and *res cogita.* Matter and the mind. Both those categories had lost some of their firmness since Maxim's college days. *Res extensa,* the notion of the solid body in physical space, had receded into the conceptual fog of modern particle physics. And *res cogita*—well, we didn't really believe in it, did we? Maxim had never been a radical reductionist, like Skinner. But it had never occurred to him to doubt that every mental event had its precise physical parallel in the brain; that a "thought" was simply a neuronal twitch of one kind or another.

Today all that had changed. Neurological science was a wasteland of warring theories; the brain was everything from a quantum-event amplifier to a chaotic equilibrium. Every step toward understanding, the discovery of this or that chemical neurotransmitter, seemed to unfold a Chinese puzzle of increasingly complex questions. Some researchers had even concluded that the effort to understand the brain was necessarily doomed—that consciousness cannot comprehend consciousness any more than a box may contain itself.

"This is really an extraordinary amount of activity," Collingwood said. "There's no question that what we have here is not a normal scan. It's all lit up—it's a bloody Christmas tree. I mean, look at the occipitals. Ordinarily, the only time you'd find that much activity is in a subject who's hallucinating." Collingwood looked over his shoulder. "*Does* he hallucinate?"

"Occasionally."

"But not just the occipitals. It's everything! He must be burning glucose at a tremendous rate."

Maxim said, "No sign of pathology?"

"Hard to say. We don't have a baseline, do we? I mean, what's it *supposed* to look like? However—" Collingwood squinted at the monitor. "There are these shadowy patches scattered through the frontal cortex. If you insist on a sign of pathology, maybe that. But I wouldn't stake a diagnosis on it." He frowned. "What did your animal studies show?"

"In a mature chimp with induced cortical growth, a decline over time. Periodic fever, convulsions, then accelerated deterioration of the induced cerebral tissue."

"Fatal?"

"Often. The decline was always permanent."

"I don't suppose you ran PETs."

"I didn't have access to a machine. You know what it's been like." Funding had dried up decades ago and the work he had performed in the fifties was still tightly classified. Following the cortical growth into maturity and old age in a primate population had been his own idea—an impulse; it would not only satisfy his curiosity, but would be useful if the publication bans were ever lifted. "We did autopsies," he told Collingwood. "The symptoms were vaguely Alzheimer's-like, but there was no specific loss of acetylcholine neurons, no neurofibrillary plaques. Our suspicion was that the new cortical growth was sufficiently distinct—in some way—that it eventually triggered an autoimmune response. Mortality depended on how essential the new growth had become to the organism."

Collingwood shook his head. "All those years ago, doing synthesis protocols—I never really imagined we would have to face this. *Him*, I mean—a human being, an enhanced adult human being. Are his symptoms severe?"

"Intermittently."

"Advanced?"

Maxim shrugged.

"Well," Collingwood said, "we might be looking at tiny lesions, peppered over the frontal lobes. But there's so much activity, Max, it's just difficult to say." He turned back to the video display. Maxim saw him stand suddenly erect as something caught his attention. "Hold on—wait a minute—"

The attending nurse in the PET room picked up a microphone; her voice was relayed to the speaker grille over Collingwood's head. "Doctor," she said, "the patient is convulsing—shall I pull him out?"

Maxim hurried to the window. He could see John lying with his head in the mouth of the PET scanner, as if he were being devoured by the machine. His pale, long limbs were trembling slightly.

Collingwood looked at Maxim; Maxim shook his head.

Collingwood said, "Hold him steady a few more minutes."

There was silence, punctuated by the whirring of disc drives. Maxim looked over Collingwood's shoulder at the video display.

The butterfly-wing image of John's brain was changing, subtly but distinctly. The bright colors began to fade; in particular, the hot band of the frontal lobes faded toward shadow. Watching, Maxim felt a cold hollowness at the pit of his stomach. "What's happening?"

"His glucose economy is suddenly down. Behaviorally, you mean? Jesus, I don't know—I've never seen anything like it."

Maxim said, "He's changing."

"That's obvious!"

"I mean, he's not John anymore. I think he's becoming Benjamin."

"The secondary personality you mentioned?"

"I believe so."

"This is radical," Collingwood said. "I've never seen this kind of bottoming-out. Is this voluntary?"

Maxim began to shake his head, then reconsidered. It was a tremendous coincidence, that Benjamin should manifest just as John was in the PET scanner. It was as if John wanted to show us this, Maxim thought. John's way of cooperating with the test.

Or Benjamin's.

"Not exactly voluntary," he told Collingwood, "not on the conscious level. But John is a unique individual. Not voluntary, but perhaps not an accident."

"The patient is febrile and convulsive," the nurse reported, "but he seems to be coming around. . . . Doctor?"

"Pull him out," Collingwood said.

He switched off the intercom and looked at Maxim. Video images were still cycling through on the monitor behind him. Cool blue butterfly wings. Icy Rorschach blots. "Jesus Christ, Max," Collingwood said tonelessly. "What did we do to this man? Just what kind of thing is he?"

16

Benjamin was back. But Benjamin had changed.

Amelie was deeply pleased, at first, to be with him again. She realized how much she had cherished the time before Benjamin went away—before Roch moved in and took his place. Having even a fraction of that life restored was like an answered prayer. She worried that there might be some conflict with Susan or Dr. Kyriakides, but there was not; aside from the time Benjamin spent in therapy sessions with Kyriakides and a few medical tests, Amelie was allowed to have him to herself. Susan maintained a polite, somber distance; and after a few days she left the city on some mission for Dr. Kyriakides.

In the beginning, Amelie was shy with him. Things had changed, after all. She knew so much more than she used to . . . maybe *too* much. She knew what Dr. Kyriakides had told her: that Benjamin was an invention of John's, a puppet creation that had somehow, like Pinocchio in the old Disney movie, come to life. She accepted that this was true; but she couldn't bring herself to believe it . . . not *really* believe it . . . certainly not when she was with Benjamin, who was, after all, a *person*, a living human being; more alive, she thought privately, than John Shaw had ever been.

But this new knowledge saddened her and made her timid; it meant that things were different now.

Mostly, she waited for Benjamin to come to her.

He did, one cold Wednesday after a therapy session with Kyriakides. Benjamin came to her room. He touched her shoulder. "Let's take a walk," he said.

———

The snow had drifted into blue mounds and dunes across the lawn. Benjamin took her by the hand and led her down the front path to a lane that wound in from the main road, along a column of snowy birches. "It's pretty here," he said.

Amelie smiled. He was always saying things like that. Simple things. She nodded.

He walked a few more paces. "You know all about me now."

"Not all about," she amended. "I wouldn't say that."

"About John and me."

"A little, I guess."

"About what I am."

She nodded.

He said, "I never lied to you, you know. But it was hard to explain."

"John wasn't around much in those days," Amelie said.

"A few nights at the doughnut shop. I remember some of that now." He looked at her somberly. "More of John's memories are spilling over. Getting mixed up with mine. Dr. Kyriakides thinks that's a good thing."

Amelie didn't respond.

"Back then," Benjamin said, "I thought he might just fade away. Otherwise—if I'd known what was going to happen—I would have told you more. I guess I thought one day he'd just be gone. There would just be me."

"It's hard to understand," Amelie ventured. "How that must feel."

"I remember a lot of John's childhood. I think those memories were always there . . . but they're closer now. I remember his time with the Woodwards. They were good people. Ordinary people. John was never what they expected—but how could he be? In a way, they were always *my* parents. Never his."

"Is it true what Kyriakides said, that John invented you?"

"That I'm a figment of his imagination?" Benjamin smiled, not altogether happily. "It doesn't feel that way."

"How *does* it feel?"

"It feels like I live inside him. It feels like I've always lived inside him. You know what 'Benjamin' means? It's an old Hebrew name. It means 'son of the left hand.' In a way, *that's* how it feels."

"You *are* left-handed," Amelie observed.

"And John's right-handed. I suppose it's true, he 'invented' me. But I think I'm more than that. Dr. Kyriakides agrees. It's like invoking a spirit. John believes he made me up, but maybe he just *found* me . . . maybe I'd been there all along, and he just opened the door and said, 'All right—come out.' "

Amelie looked at Benjamin with dismay—not because of what he said, which seemed true and obvious, but because of the way he said it.

Benjamin had never talked about himself this way. It wasn't like him.

He's different, Amelie thought.

He's changing.

———

She went to his bed that night, cuddled with him under the blankets. The furnace was roaring away in the basement, but this old house was hard to heat. She liked his warmth; she liked being held.

They made love. But when he was inside her, and she was looking up at him, at his big eyes strangely radiant in the dim light, Amelie felt suddenly afraid. She could not explain it, even to herself. It was not just the fear that he might be John, or partly John. It was the *depth* of his eyes. She was afraid of what she might see there. Something unfamiliar. Something she would not recognize. Something no one would ever recognize.

Afterward, she slept with her back to him. He curled around her with his arm across her belly, and her apprehension vanished into sleep.

————

Really, she had been living with two men all along, John and Benjamin. The thing was that she had never admitted it to herself.

She would wake up some mornings with a stranger beside her. She always knew at once when John was manifesting. He looked different; he had a different face. But he manifested seldom, and she had learned to anticipate his appearances. Even so, inevitably, there were times when she would wake up and find John in bed with her; and then she would feel frightened and confused. It was nothing she could ever explain to anyone. It was not a topic that came up on Donahue—"What to do when your lover is actually two people!" There was no one she had even tried to explain it to —except Susan, who was a special case. But Susan, when you came right down to it, was a pampered California preppie who could not help condescending even when she tried to be Amelie's friend. Amelie forgave this . . . it was predictable . . . but she despaired of any real contact. Besides, Susan was obviously messed up over John.

So I'm alone.

Amelie awoke with this bleak thought echoing in her head. She turned and regarded the face of the man beside her. It was Benjamin. Absolutely no question. But the uneasiness lingered. She stood up, pulled her nightgown on, walked back down the silent corridor to the room Dr. Kyriakides had assigned to her.

There was a little Sanyo stereo they'd bought to replace the one Roch had trashed. Amelie slid a Doors tape into the player and plugged the headphones into the jack. The tape was *L.A. Woman.* She boosted the volume and flopped down onto the bed.

Thinking of Benjamin. Thinking of last summer, when they'd been together—before Roch, before Susan. Hot days in that crummy little apartment. Hot nights.

Thinking of wrapping her legs around him. Of his weight against her . . . of his gentleness, even when he was close to coming. Of the way he laid his hand alongside her cheek, intimate as a kiss.

Thinking of his eyes.

Wondering where she would go . . . because it was over, wasn't it? No way to crank back the seasons. No way to make it be new again.

Morrison performed his familiar death wail. The sound seemed to come from inside her head. She reached over to slide the volume up but her hand slipped and she hit the *reject* button instead. The tape popped out. The silence was eerie and sudden.

She went to the window and stood gazing out, without music or thoughts . . . as empty as she could make herself, watching the snow fall.

———

Dr. Kyriakides: Do you remember your childhood?

Benjamin: Yes.

Kyriakides: But it *wasn't* your childhood.

Benjamin: It was a shadow. I remember faces. I remember moments. Is it so different for everyone else?

Kyriakides: You were another person then.

Benjamin: No. That doesn't make sense. I can't say, 'I was John.' I was there all along . . . *with* him. In the shadows.

Kyriakides: And then you came into the light.

Benjamin: Yes.

Kyriakides: When he created you.

Benjamin: If you say so.

Kyriakides: You were always yourself—is that how it seems?

Benjamin: I was always myself. I came into the light, I lived at home. I went to school. Then I was back in the dark awhile. And then I woke up and I was on the island, John's island. I knew what he'd been doing and why he was there.

Kyriakides: And why *you* were there?

Benjamin: I knew that, too. [Pause.] You have to understand, it was the end of his road. He'd gone as far as he could. [Pause.] He wanted to die, but he didn't want to kill himself.

Kyriakides: I can't imagine John saying that.

Benjamin: Oh, he would never say it. Especially not to you. He doesn't trust you. He's never forgiven you.

Kyriakides: For making him what he is?

Benjamin: For leaving him alone.

Kyriakides: But surely—it's possible now that he *is* dying. And yet he fights it.

Benjamin: The funny thing is that he's changed his mind. He thinks maybe there *is* a reason to go on living.

Kyriakides: Can you tell me that reason?

Benjamin: No.

Kyriakides: He doesn't want you to.

Benjamin: Right.

Kyriakides: You know that about him?

Benjamin: I know a lot of things about him.

Kyriakides: Have you always known these things?

Benjamin: Known them, maybe. Never thought about them much. Never used to do this much thinking!

Kyriakides: Is that because of the way you're changing?

Benjamin: Could be. [Another pause.] He's all through me now, you know. We're sort of mixed together. There used to be a kind of wall. But that's breaking down.

Kyriakides: Well, I think that's good, Benjamin. I think that needs to happen.

Benjamin: Well, it isn't easy for him. He's fighting it.

Kyriakides: That's unfortunate. Why is he fighting it?

Benjamin: The same reason he wanted to die, back on the island. Because he hates me. Didn't you know that? He hates all of us. [A longer pause.] Almost all.

———

Benjamin came into the room while Amelie was packing.

Amelie ignored him—just went on emptying the big chest of drawers into her ragged Salvation Army suitcase, pretending he wasn't there.

After a time, watching her, he said, "Where will you go?"

It was a very Benjamin thing to say. Straight to the point, no bullshit, kind of little-boy innocent. It reminded her of what she had loved about him and what she still loved, and that was painful; she winced. She looked up at him. "I don't know. Maybe back to Montreal. It doesn't matter."

He said, "I wish you wouldn't go."

She turned to the window. The snow was still falling. Fucking horrible winter. That was the thing about winter in this city. It was likely to do any fucking thing. If you were ready for snow you got rain; if you were ready for rain you got ice. "I thought you understood."

"You're leaving me."

She turned to him. "So? You left me."

"No. John left you."

"But you were talking about leaving. Even before that. And when you finally called, you called Susan."

He shrugged, as if to say: Yes, that's so.

She said, "Things had already started to change, hadn't they?

Even then. You knew we couldn't stay together. You knew what was happening." He did not answer, which was answer enough. Amelie nodded. "Yeah—you knew."

"I know a lot of things I don't want to know. A lot of it is John. There's more John now than there used to be." His frown was huge. "I wish you would stay a while longer."

"Why?"

"Because it's cold out. Because you don't have anywhere to go." That helpless look. "Because there's nothing anyone can do about this, about what's happening to me."

Amelie narrowed her eyes. "How do you know?"

"John knows. Kyriakides was lying all along. He lied to Susan about it. But John can tell. Kyriakides wanted to do the tests, and maybe he thought there was a chance that something would happen, something miraculous. But there's nothing. He knows it, John knows it. That's not why they're here."

"Why, then?"

"Kyriakides is here to finish his experiment, and because he feels guilty. John is here—well, it's an experiment of his own. But for me, I think it's only the end. I'm scared of that."

"Goddammit, Benjamin!"

She held out her arms for him. He put his head against her shoulder.

She was blinking away tears. But who was she sorry for? Herself or him? Maybe both of us, Amelie thought. Two fucked-up losers. She just felt so *sad*.

"Nothing is the way it used to be," he said. "I love you."

"I'll stay a while longer," Amelie said. "It'll be okay."

Not believing either of these things.

———

After some time had passed he helped her unpack again. He was about to leave the room when he reached into his back pocket and said, "Almost forgot—this came for you today."

It was a thick manila envelope bearing the return address of the Goodtime Grill on Yonge Street.

He held it out.

Amelie took it from him, frowning.

17

After the humiliation involving his sister, Roch had checked himself in at the Family Practice Clinic at Toronto General Hospital. A few days later and he might have run into Amelie while she was in town for John's PET scan. But he wasn't looking for Amelie—at least, not yet.

His chest was a mass of bruises where the car door had slammed into it. The clinic sent him up for X-rays, but there was no evidence of any significant fracture to the ribs, which was good; it meant he wouldn't have to be taped. Hurt like shit all the same, though. The doctor, a woman about as tall as Roch's collarbone, asked whether he'd been in a fight. He said, "A fight with a fucking Honda."

In return she flashed him a skeptical, condescending look . . . which burned, but Roch kept carefully silent; this was not the place or the time. He was getting older, developing an instinct for these things—when to hold his tongue and when to act. He

merely stared into the female doctor's wide green eyes until she
frowned and looked away. Roch smiled to himself.

She cleared her throat. "Warm baths might help with that
bruising. Maybe Tylenol for the pain. You'll be fine in a couple of
weeks. If you stay away from Hondas."

"It wasn't a joke."

"What?"

"About the Honda. It wasn't a joke."

"No . . . I guess it wasn't." She bowed her head and made a
notation in his file folder. "Is there anything else?"

Roch stood up and left the office.

—————

The landlady had wanted to kick him out of Amelie's apartment,
but she backed off when he paid two months rent in cash and
promised to clean the place up. He told her he was working as a
clerk for the provincial government. Which was a lie, of course;
he'd picked up the rent money doing day labor. His life savings,
ha-ha. The fucking check had taken two weeks to clear, or else
he'd have spent it by now. But it was important to have a place to
sleep.

Though he hated being alone.

It was getting harder all the time.

At night, especially. With Amelie gone he didn't have to sleep
on the sofa, but the bedroom was like a big box with its single
square, soot-darkened window. He would lie awake in this cold,
dark room and feel the city pressing in at him. The city made a
noise, as familiar as his own heartbeat but more disturbing. Sirens,
motors, tires gritting down cold night streets. This noise was amplified by the winter air and beat against Roch's eardrums until he
could not distinguish it from the singing of the radiators or the
rush of his own blood.

He resented the sound. It was the sound of everything he could
not have: pleasure, companionship, confidence. He couldn't walk
those streets except as an outcast. He had learned that lesson

when he was very young. Nowadays he did not attract much im-
mediate attention; he was older and less physically grotesque; he
worked out in the gym. He was not the puddingy, froglike thing
he had been as a child. But he was not one of those ordinary
people, either. He could not move among these handsome men
and confident, smiling women except as an impostor. He might
have been a creature from outer space, disguised as human. He
knew that.

He was alone in the dark and his ribs hurt and he had been
humiliated.

And he was angry.

He thought about getting drunk. But, oddly, the impulse wasn't
really there. When he thought about drinking he pictured his
father coming home on winter nights like this, screaming out
curses in peasant French and beating Roch with his stubby fists.
Big man's hands with dark hair and callused knuckles: Roch remembered those hands.

Lying in bed, he looked at his own right-hand fist—a shadow in
the dim light. It was his best friend, his lover, the instrument of
justice.

His anger was like a cold, uncomfortable stone that had lodged
in his chest.

And he understood, then, why he didn't want to get drunk.
This was a pressure that drinking would not have relieved. He
needed all his energy for planning, because he was going to fucking *do something* about this thing with Amelie. Roch understood
revenge in intricate detail. The rules were basic. When you were
humiliated, you had to eat it—or else enforce a punishment. And
he knew all about punishment. Punishment was like a big, simple
machine. It was easy to operate once you got it going, and terribly
difficult to stop. And all it took to work that machine was some
careful planning.

And he was good at that. It was the only kind of abstract
thinking Roch enjoyed. It shut out the night sounds of the city.

He could spend hours working out the details and the necessary steps, the payoff being some act . . . it was not yet specific . . . some final and irretrievable moment of equalization. An orgasm of justice.

This new purpose seemed to seize him all at once, utterly.

He was not smart, but he had a goal. And he was methodical. And determined. And perhaps best of all, he knew a secret. He thought of all those people out there in the lively darkness of the city, thought about how they were bound to one another with sticky ropes of loyalty, love, duty, guilt—how these impediments constrained them and restricted their movement. And Roch smiled in the dark, because here was his deepest and most profound knowledge about himself: that he was not bound by any of these things. He could do things that ordinary people could not even imagine. He was utterly alone, and therefore he was utterly free.

The first step was to locate Amelie.

He had never been to the restaurant where she used to work, the Goodtime Grill, mainly because her employment there had always rankled him. It was scutwork and she deserved it, but it had given her an independence from him that Roch resented deeply. This was back when they were on the street, when she was shaving her hair and wearing that old leather jacket with the sleeves down over her hands so that only her fingers poked out, how whorish she had looked and how she resented it when he suggested the logical and obvious way of bringing in some money. As if she *liked* sleeping in abandoned buildings, for Christ's sake. He savored for a moment the memory of her in that jacket and how the cars would cruise by and sometimes stop and men would call her over and how she would come back sometimes with a little money and that expression on her face, which he could not decipher—of some deep, secret grief. But then she got the restaurant job and the crappy St. Jamestown apartment, and Roch got involved with some guys boosting cars out in the suburbs, and he forgot about her for a while. That was the basic mistake he'd made—letting her get away from him.

So he'd never been inside this particular restaurant. But maybe that was a good thing. Nobody here would know him.

He stood a second on the Yonge Street sidewalk staring up at the "Goodtime" sign. Cold noon sun on cheap faded plastic, picture windows with bead curtains and a menu taped up: Souvlaki, Fish & Chips, Burger Platter. Roch pushed his way through the door.

He took a table by the window. This was the hard part, he thought. Anything involving deception was difficult for him. He could not predict what people would say, and the things *he* said often provoked strange, hostile reactions. But there was no need to hurry. This was only the first, the most basic step.

One of the waitresses brought him water. She was a tiny small-breasted woman who looked vaguely Oriental. According to the tag on her uniform, her name was TRACY. In a voice so timorous he barely made out the words, she asked him if he was ready to order.

He asked for the burger plate and a beer.

When she came back with the food, he said, "Tracy—is that your name?"

She ducked her head, which Roch took for a nod.

He said, "Tracy, listen, is Amelie around?"

"Oh—Amelie? Oh—she doesn't work here anymore."

"I'm sorry. I didn't know that."

"Are you one of her regulars? 'Cause I don't recognize you. But I've only been here since summer."

"I'm her brother," Roch said.

He watched her face carefully. She narrowed her eyes and tensed up a little. Obviously this information meant something to her. Amelie had been talking.

Loudmouthed bitch.

But Roch felt a tingle of excitement.

"Oh, her brother, okay," Tracy said, and turned away. Roch let her go. Slowly now, he instructed himself. He forced himself to eat, even though he wasn't hungry. The food was tasteless; it had the texture of styrofoam.

When Tracy came back with his coffee, Roch smiled at her. "You a friend of Amelie's?"

"I can't talk," she said. Her voice sounded like it had died in her throat. "I have other tables."

"I know I haven't been on good terms with her. Maybe she mentioned that? The thing is, she's gone off and I don't know where to find her."

Tracy only stared at him, the carafe somewhat slack in her hands.

"Look, I'm not trying to hassle her. Is that the problem? You don't have to tell me where she is. The thing is that I have some of her stuff. Mail and things like that. She didn't leave a forwarding address. I just want to know whether, if I gave you some of this stuff, you could maybe get it to her."

There was a long, delicate silence.

"I don't know," Tracy said finally.

But Roch had to struggle to contain his excitement, because this was all the confirmation he needed. Tracy knew how to find Amelie. Otherwise she would have said, "No," or "I'm sorry."

But he was improvising now. He didn't really have a plan; only the glimmer of a possibility—an idea beginning to take shape at the back of his head. "Look," he said, "if I packaged up some of this stuff and left it with you—would that be all right?"

"And bring it here to the restaurant?" Tracy said. "Because I can't give out my address or anything."

Christ, Roch thought, she thinks I'm after *her!* It was laughable. He imagined pinning down this goggle-eyed bitch and raping her. It was a joke. But some of the thought must have been reflected in his eyes or his expression, because she took a sudden, startled step backward. He restored his smile and aimed it at Tracy again. "Sure, I can bring the stuff here."

"Well, maybe, I don't know," Tracy said, and put down the check and scurried away.

Roch left his money and a generous tip and went out into the street. He walked aimlessly for a while, breathing frost into the cold air. Really, this was turning out terrifically well. But he still had a lot of thinking to do.

———

Some days passed while he pondered the problem of extracting Amelie's whereabouts from Tracy the waitress.

Roch approached the problem by stocking up on food, mainly TV dinners, and holing up in the apartment. He kept the television turned on, and insulated the windows with strips of hardware-store foam, so that the apartment absorbed as much heat as possible from the building's big, laboring oil furnace. The combination of the dry heat and the staticky noise of the TV helped him think. Ideas came to him in harsh, glaring staccato, like commercials.

He thought about using force to extract the information from Tracy. Follow her home one of these nights. Beat it out of her, choke it out of her, whatever. She was scared of him already; it wouldn't be hard.

But it would be messy and it might get him in trouble. Even worse—unless he could frighten her into silence—she might be able to warn Amelie. Dangerous.

But how else?

He was frustrated, thinking about it. He did a set of pushups, ate a frozen dinner, and watched a *Movie of the Week* on TV. Nothing. He went to bed.

Inspiration came with the morning mail.

He had begun collecting Amelie's mail, what there was of it, in case he needed it to flesh out the story he'd told at the Goodtime. The problem was that his sister had been getting junk mail and subscription ads and dunning letters from the credit department of a downtown department store, but not much else—not the sort of thing anyone would go out of his way to pass on.

Today, however, there was an envelope with an illegible return address and a Montreal postmark . . . and Roch, sensing its importance, sat down to think before he tried to open it.

Amelie's name and address were written in an arthritic scrawl across the front. Think, he instructed himself. Who did she know in Montreal? Somebody from school? But Amelie hadn't been that tight with friends. Anyway, it looked like an old woman's writing.

"Jesus," Roch said out loud. "Mama?"

He held the letter in his hand as if it were a religious relic. The letter was important. It was the key. Roch was suddenly, intuitively certain of that. He could use this letter to pry Amelie out of her hiding place . . . somehow . . . but he had to be cautious; he had to make plans.

He deliberately set aside the letter and watched TV for a while. He couldn't concentrate, of course. Morning game shows flickered and vanished; the news came on. He forced his eyes to focus on the screen. It was an exercise in discipline.

The question occurred to him: was it really possible to *steam open* a letter?

He had heard about "steaming open" mail. But he had no idea how to go about it. And, of course, he couldn't risk destroying the letter itself.

He went to the kitchen and filled the kettle, put it on the stove to boil. While he waited he went through the mail he'd been collecting and selected three pieces: a book-club flyer, a phone bill, and a sweepstakes ad. All three were addressed to Amelie; all three were sealed. He cradled them in his hand, thinking hard.

The kettle whistled as it came up to steam. It was a hard, shrill whistle but Roch didn't mind; he liked the sound. He took the book-club flyer and grasped it in a pair of kitchen tongs, then held it so that the gummed flap took the brunt of the steam. He held it there while thirty seconds ticked off on his wristwatch.

He realized as soon as he pulled it away that this had been a mistake; the envelope was a sodden mass. He waved it in the air to cool it and then tried the flap. The glue had been steamed away, sure enough. But the paper was drenched.

He tried again with the phone bill. This time he passed the envelope quickly through the steam, a little farther from the spout. He managed not to damage the paper, but the glue was still firm. After a second pass he was able to pry up an edge without tearing anything. A third pass and the envelope peeled open in his hand; it was damp but would probably dry to its original condition.

He practiced again on the sweepstakes flyer and did a little better this time. He figured he had the hang of it.

Now the letter from Montreal.

He carried it carefully into the kitchen and set it on the counter. He dried the tongs and then grasped the envelope. The kettle was still screaming. He turned to center it on the burner and then—disaster!—the Montreal letter slipped through the pincer-end of the tongs toward a sink full of dirty dishwater. "Shit!" Roch screamed. He clenched the tongs convulsively and managed to catch a corner of the envelope; it dangled over the water until he could snatch it away with his free hand.

His heart was beating a mile a minute. He forced himself to stand still, calm down.

The kettle continued to shriek, inches from his ear.

He took a deep breath and started again.

The second time was lucky. It worked like a charm. He worried out the letter from the envelope, unfolded it, and sat down to read.

The kettle dried up and fell silent. Roch stood up to turn the heat off, but too late: the cheap aluminum was red hot and brittle. He threw the kettle in the sink, where it hissed and generated a white, astringent-smelling cloud. The kitchen was already tropical; the whole apartment was as humid as a hothouse. He imagined spores taking root in the old wallpaper, fungus breaking out in the dark corners of these narrow rooms. He was troubled by this thought, but only briefly. He sat down and concentrated on the letter. He had important things to do.

———

The letter was typewritten, pecked out on an ancient, faded ribbon. Roch had a hard time reconciling the text with his memories of his mother. Mama was a big woman who had often been drunk and sometimes aggressive. One time he'd seen her get into a fight with a shoe clerk at Ogilvy's—she tore a flap of skin off the guy's cheek. Whereas this letter was a whining, pathetic document, mainly about the lousy neighborhood she was forced to live in and how long it had been since Amelie wrote back.

Screw the old bitch, Roch thought. She never wrote to *me*.

But the bulk of his plan was already beginning to take its final shape. It was a grand, glowing edifice, and he was its architect. A brace here, a capstone there. He smiled and set the letter aside.

In the afternoon he rode a bus down to the Salvation Army thrift shop and spent ten dollars on a clapped-out Underwood Noiseless typewriter. He took it home and discovered that the ribbon wouldn't advance, but that he could produce legible copy if he cranked the spool by hand every line or two. He typed *The quick brown fox* and compared this with the letter from Mama.

The specimen was similar but far from identical. Still, Roch thought, who notices these things? He doubted that Amelie would have an older letter to compare it with or that she would bother if she did, as long as the counterfeit seemed authentic.

He inserted a piece of plain white bond into the Underwood and sat before it, sweating. He could not think of a way to begin . . . then realized that he could copy Mama's letter as written, with a few critical amendments of his own. He smiled at the ingenuity of this and began pecking.

The cap came off the "e" key before he was finished, but he managed to wangle it back on without too much mess. He typed the penultimate paragraph from the original, then dropped the "you never write" complaints and added:

Because I want to see you I have bouhgt bus tickets to Toronto and will be ariving Saturday Feb 10. Hope you can meet me at the Bus Station as I do not know how to findyour Apartment exactly. I would call you but unfortuntly the Phone has been take out again by those Bastards at the Phone Co.

Roch sat back and smiled at this, especially the bit about the telephone, which not only solved a potential problem but sounded a lot like Mama. He typed,

Your Loving Mother,

and duplicated her signature with a blue Bic pen.

Masterpiece.

The only remaining problem was re-sealing the envelope. Amelie had left a jar of mucilage in the kitchen drawer, and Roch discovered that a very thin layer of this would pass for the original glue. He sealed the envelope and set it aside. Good enough for today. He turned on the TV and watched *Wheel of Fortune,* content with the state of the world.

———

On his way back to the Goodtime Grill the next morning, a troubling thought occurred to him:

What if Amelie didn't take the bait?

There was no love lost between those two, after all. Roch did not hate either of his parents—except his father, sporadically; hating them was a waste of time. But he knew that Amelie harbored deeper feelings, mostly negative. Amelie sometimes talked about Mama sympathetically, but with her fists clenched and her nails digging into her palms. Maybe she wouldn't show up at the bus depot.

Or maybe—another new thought—she was too far away. Maybe she'd left the city. She might be in fucking Timbuctoo, although Roch suspected not; it wasn't her style. But who knew? Anything was possible.

No, he thought, better not to borrow trouble. If the letter arrangement fell through, he'd try something else. He had the connection through Tracy; that was secure and that was enough for now.

Tracy recognized him when he sat down at the table by the window. He saw her say something to the manager, who looked impatient and sent her scooting over with a glass of water and the order pad. Roch smiled his biggest smile and ordered lunch. When she came back with the food he reached into his jacket pocket, very casually, and brought out a wad of mail including the spiked envelope.

"I remembered to bring these," he said. "Thought maybe you'd want to pass 'em on."

Tracy took the envelopes but held them at a distance, as if they might be radioactive. "Oh," she said. "Well, okay, I'll see what I can do, okay?"

"If it's convenient," Roch said.

"Oh," Tracy said.

———

One more thing, one more small item to take care of, and then he'd be ready. Everything would be in place.

That night he walked down Wellesley to the corner where Tony Morriseau, the drug dealer, was hanging out.

Roch didn't know Tony too well. Roch didn't believe in doing drugs; drugs fucked up your mind. He had, admittedly, sometimes scored a little of this or that from Tony, when the inclination took him or he wanted to impress somebody. But he was not a regular customer.

Tony stood on the snowy streetcorner done up in a khaki green parka with a big hood, his breath steaming out in clouds. He regarded Roch from this sheltered space with an expression Roch could not decipher. Tony seemed more paranoid these days, Roch had observed.

Tony rubbed his hands together and said, "It's fucking cold, so tell me what you want."

"Something serious," Roch said.

"Speak English," Tony said.

Roch mimed the act of holding a hypodermic needle against his arm and pressing the plunger.

Tony looked ill. "Christ," he said, "don't do that, all right? You don't know who's looking." He seemed to withdraw into the depths of the parka. "I don't deal with that."

"You know where to get it," Roch said.

"Matter of fact I don't."

"If you can't sell it to me, tell me who can."

"I don't like your tone of voice," Tony said. "I don't have to do you any favors. Christ!"

Roch stood up straight and looked down at Tony, who was at least a head shorter. "Tone of voice?"

Tony cringed.

Then Tony looked at his watch. "Oh, well . . . from now on you don't come to me for this. Go to the source, okay? It's really not my territory."

Roch nodded.

They walked down the street to Tony's car—a battered Buick. "Hey, Tony," Roch said. "What happened to the famous Corvette?"

Tony scowled and shook his head. "You don't want to know."

18

It was a cool Southern California winter day, but Susan was comfortable with a sweater wrapped around her. She was able to stand for a long time on the exposed, sunny hillside where her father was buried.

She had been given a week-long leave of absence from the big house north of Toronto and she wasn't sure whether to resent this or not. Dr. Kyriakides had practically hustled her onto the airplane, claimed that the trip would be good for her, that she had driven herself to the point of nervous exhaustion—that "Benjamin" would probably be around for a while longer and there was nothing helpful she could do. "We'll need you more later," he said. During the crisis, he meant. When John's neurological breakdown reached its apex.

But no one could say for sure when that crisis would come, or what the final resolution might be. Therefore, Susan thought, it was a terrible risk to be away from him. But Dr. Kyriakides had been persuasive . . . and it was true that she owed her mother a visit. Susan had promised at the funeral that she would be home every Christmas. A promise she'd broken this year.

So she had spent five days in this quiet suburb, driving to the malls with her sixty-five-year-old mother and dodging questions about her work. She said she was doing "an exchange project" with the University of Toronto, to explain her Canadian address. Fluid transfer in mitochondria. Too complex to explain. Her mother nodded dubiously.

And today—the last day of Susan's visit—they had come here to this grave, where Susan had stood frowning for the last forty-five minutes, poised on the brink of a mystery.

She was distressed to discover that she could not summon up a concrete image of her father. She tried and failed. She could remember only the things she associated with him—his clothes, the mirror polish on his shoes, the brown sample cases he had carried to work. The rest was either hopelessly vague or, worse, deathbed images, his emaciated body and hollow eyes. She remembered the sound of his voice, the soothing rumble of it, but that was a childhood memory. His laryngeal cancer had ended all that, of course; but it seemed to Susan that he had fallen mute years before the operation, a functional silence in which anything meaningful must never be pronounced. His way of protecting her from the divorce, from his own fears, from adulthood. She was trying hard not to hate him for it.

How awful that sounded. But it was true: she had never forgiven him for his silence, for his cancer, for his callous descent into the grave. It was a monumentally selfish thought. A *childish* thought . . . but maybe that was the heart of the matter: she could never come to this place *except* as a child, suspended in time by his withdrawal and his death. She would never be his "grown-up daughter." She couldn't say any of the things she needed to say, because he couldn't listen.

She was startled by the touch of her mother's hand on her shoulder.

"Come on, Susan. We've been here long enough."

Have we? Susan climbed into the car dutifully, a child, thinking: *Maybe not.* Maybe if she stayed long enough, the right words would come to her. Talking to herself, she would talk to Daddy. And Daddy would answer. His buried words would rise up from the ground and hover in the cool, sunlit air.

But she couldn't stay forever. And so the car carried her down the hillside in the long light of the afternoon, away from the stubbornly silent ground.

———

Her flight out of Los Angeles left an hour and forty minutes late, which meant she missed her connection at O'Hare. The next available seat to Toronto was on a red-eye flight; she had an afternoon and evening to kill in Chicago.

She phoned Toronto with this news and then—on an impulse —rented a car for the day. She did not want to stray too far from the airport; Susan distrusted official scheduling and usually preferred to lurk near the departure gates. But she knew her way around this city and she recalled that John's old neighborhood, the neighborhood where he had grown up with the Woodwards, was only a short drive from the airport.

Winter hadn't affected the city too severely. There was a glaze of snow along the highway embankments, but the air was clear, with faint trails of wintery cirrus clouds running down to a powder blue horizon. But it was cold, the kind of cold that made the tires crackle against the blacktop.

She had written down John's old address in her notebook. The neighborhood was a Levittown, a postwar bungalow suburb, treeless and bleak in the winter light. She located the street—a cul-de-sac—and then the house, a pastel pink box indistinguishable from any of these others. THE WOODWARDS was printed on the mailbox. A sign posted on the front lawn said FOR SALE and a smaller one beside it announced a CONTENTS SALE—SATURDAY FEBRUARY 16.

Today.

Susan allowed the car to drift to a stop.

She didn't think she would have the courage, but she did: she got out of the car and walked up the driveway and knocked on the door, shivering. She was about to turn away when the door opened a crack and a grey-haired, chunky man peered out.

"Mr. Woodward?"

"Yes?"

She took a breath. "I, uh—I saw the sign—"

"Sale ended at four o'clock," he said, swinging the door wider, "but you might as well come in. Hardly anybody else showed up."

Susan stepped inside.

The house had obviously been stripped down for moving. There were blank spaces where there should have been furniture, and curtain rods empty over the windows. It seemed to Susan that James Woodward had been similarly stripped down. He was not as big as she had pictured him; not nearly as imposing. He was a small, barrel-chested man with a fringe of grey hair and big, callused hands. He was friendly but distant, and Susan was careful to pretend an interest in this item or that as he conducted her in and out of these small rooms. What she really wanted was to find some ghost of John or even Benjamin lingering here; but there was nothing like that . . . only these mute, empty spaces. Coming down the stairs she said, "Is your wife home?" He shook his head. "She died. That's why I'm moving. I tried looking after this place for a while, but it's too big for one person." He opened the basement door. "There's a few things still stored down here—if you think it's worth the look."

"Please," Susan said.

This was where his workshop had been, though most of the tools had been carried away. Not much left—a battered workbench with curls of pine and cedar still nesting under it; an ancient P.A. amplifier with its tubes pulled. In one shadowy corner, an acoustic guitar.

Susan went to it immediately.

"Oh, that," Woodward said. "You don't want that."

"Maybe I do," Susan said.

"You know, I sold some guitars earlier. I used to make 'em by hand. Like a hobby I guess you could say. But that one—see, the truss rod's off true. You know guitars? Well, it means it'll go off tune and be hard to fix. The action's a little too high off the frets, too. It's a bad instrument."

"How much do you want for it?"

"Say, fifty bucks for the materials? If you're serious. You play?"

"No," Susan said. "But I have a friend who does." She took the money out of her purse.

James Woodward accepted the payment; Susan picked up the guitar. It was heavier than she expected. The strings rang faintly under her fingers.

"I almost hate to sell the damn thing," Woodward said. He looked past Susan, past these walls. "It's funny," he said. "It's the broken things that stay on your mind. Broken, bent, half-made or bad-made. You take them to the grave with you."

———

She climbed off the plane in Toronto weary and dazed, collected her suitcase and the guitar from the baggage carousel. Dr. Kyriakides was waiting in the crowded space beyond the customs checkpoint.

She understood by his hollow smile that something was wrong. She followed him up to the carpark and loaded her baggage into the trunk of the Honda, daunted by his silence.

"John is back," he said finally.

"That's good," Susan responded.

Dr. Kyriakides opened the car door for her. Ever the European gentleman.

"But Amelie is missing," he said.

19

It was a long drive back to the house. A snowstorm had settled in from the west and wasn't leaving; the car radio warned people to stay off the roads. Susan was grateful that Dr. Kyriakides had been able to maneuver the Honda all the way to the airport; she was even more grateful that she was able to drive it back. Visibility had closed in and the road was blanked out north of the city; the headlights probed into a swirling wilderness. For the time, she was too preoccupied with driving to press for details about Amelie.

The weather grew steadily worse, but the tires were good and there wasn't much traffic and they were back at the house before long. Kyriakides brushed the snow from the car while Susan headed for the kitchen and a hot cup of coffee.

John was there, waiting for her.

It was John—no doubt about it.

He looked up as she came through the door. His expression was somber and utterly focused.

"I need to do two things," he said. "First, I need to talk to you. There are a lot of things I want to say while I still can."

Susan nodded solemnly. She was too tired to be shocked by this sudden volley; she simply accepted it. "Second?"

He said, "I mean to find Amelie."

———

Susan slept for five dreamless hours between three and eight o'clock in the morning.

She woke to find the window of her room laced with frost. She stood for a moment, touching the icy surface of the glass with one finger and wondering at the intensity of the cold. Outside, the world was a blurred grey-white wilderness. The snow had obscured the driveway. The highway was empty save for a plough inching southward under its strange blue safety light. The sky was dark and the snow was falling steadily. She dressed in the darkness of her room.

She carried her portable Sony tape recorder down the hall to John's door, raised her hand to knock—and then paused.

John was playing the guitar. She had given him the instrument last night, had explained about the layover in Chicago and the sale at the Woodward house. He had taken the instrument wordlessly, his expression unreadable.

The music came softly through the closed door. He was good, Susan thought. She didn't recognize the piece—something baroque. Not passionate music but subtle, a sad melody elaborated into a cathedral of notes. She waited until the last arpeggio had faded away.

He put down the guitar when she came through the door, looked questioningly at the tape recorder.

"It's for me," she said. "I don't trust myself to remember."

He nodded. She felt his sense of urgency: it was like something physical, a third presence in the room. Because of his impending neurological crisis, Susan thought, his "change"—or because of Amelie. Or both.

He's changed. He's different.

But she put the thought aside for now.

"Sit down," John said.

She plugged a cassette into the recorder and switched it on.

———

All that morning he talked about his childhood.

They skipped breakfast. Twice, Susan paused to change tapes. She was afraid she would miss something. It was a fear John didn't share, obviously. The words poured out of him like water from a broken jug. A cataract of words.

She understood what he was doing. He had explained it to her last night. These were things he had never said, small but vital fragments of his life, and he was afraid they would slip away uncommunicated. She was not expected to learn these things verbatim or play them back to him—the tape recorder was superfluous. It was the telling that mattered. "Nothing is permanent," John said. "Everything is volatile. You, me, the world—*everything.* But it's like throwing a stone into a pool of water. The stone disappears. But the ripples linger awhile."

She was that pool. He was the stone.

———

He talked about his mother.

Her name was Marga Novak and she was working through her apprenticeship at a hairdressing salon in downtown Chicago when she answered a classified ad in the back pages of the *Tribune:* "Pregnant, single women wanted for privately funded medical study."

She had recently become pregnant by a thirty-five-year-old shingle and siding salesman who had promised to marry her but who left town, or was relocated, a couple of weeks after she announced the results of the pregnancy test. For Marga, answering the *Trib* ad was a last resort. But the salon was sure to fire her when she started to show, and she needed some kind of income.

She passed two screening interviews and was introduced to Dr.

Kyriakides, who explained that the treatment—to prevent low birthweight and "give the child a healthy start"—might involve some discomfort in connection with the intrauterine injections but would be perfectly safe for both mother and child. Moreover, the follow-up study would include a fully paid private educational program for the baby and ongoing medical care for both of them. In the meantime all expenses would be taken care of and housing would be arranged.

She agreed, of course. Was there a choice? The injections were uncomfortable but the delivery was easy, even allowing for the infant's exaggerated cranial size. Mother and child were installed in a two-bedroom town house near the university district, and John's schooling began almost immediately.

———

"How do you know all this?" Susan asked.

"I broke into Max's office one night. Came in from the Woodwards' house in the suburbs. I was twelve years old. He kept his files and his notes in a little vault behind his desk. I'd seen it there a few years before. I'd seen him open it."

"After all that time? You remembered the combination?"

John nodded and continued.

———

Marga's parents were Czechs who had come to America before the war. She hadn't spoken to her mother or father for fifteen years; she didn't know whether they were still alive. This baby was in effect her only family.

Marga understood soon enough that John was a special child. Even the name "John"—she hadn't chosen it herself. It had been Dr. Kyriakides' suggestion. The doctor was polite but firm and Marga acquiesced because she was afraid of offending him. He paid all the bills, after all. In a very real sense, he owned her.

She hardly saw the baby. She tried to be a responsible mother, at least at first. But there were research people always coming to take the child away. He slept in a crib in Marga's room most nights; they had that time together. But the doctors must have been doing something to him, she thought—something she didn't understand.

He was a *strange* child.

He began talking too soon—at only a few months! But more than that. She sensed it every time she picked him up . . . every time she put him to her breast. There was a discomfort she once described to Dr. Kyriakides as something like the sound of a piano string gone off tune. ("Dissonance," Kyriakides supplied.) And the baby's eyes were too observant.

It wasn't like touching a baby, she said. It was like touching . . . a dwarf.

After that confession, she saw even less of John. Marga pretended that this made her unhappy, but really it didn't. . . . It was nice, having some time to herself for a change.

————

"I remember Max more clearly than I remember Marga. Marga is just a face. Small eyes. Big body, big shapeless dresses. She wore a perfume that smelled like linden flowers. Overpowering!

"Max was different then. He had more hair. A heavy Joe Stalin moustache and rimless glasses. It was frightening. I trusted him, of course. He was the central force, the operating engine. It was obvious that everything revolved around him, everybody followed his orders.

"He taught me more than anyone else. I had plenty of professional tutors. But it was Max who would really talk to me. If I asked a question, he took it seriously. Child questions, you know: how high is the sky and what comes *after* it? But he understood that I didn't want trivial answers. I wanted the true answers.

"And there was the way he looked at me.

"You have to understand how the others treated me. The other research staff, even Marga. I would sit at a little table and they would run a Stanford-Binet or a Thematic Aperception and after a while they would start to register their disbelief—or their fear, or their resentment. I was strange, anomalous, different. I was scary. I learned to recognize it—I thought of it as 'The Look.' After I was a year old, Marga would never touch me, never wanted to pick me up. And when she did: The Look.

"But Max was different. Max knew what I was. Took *pride* in me. That meant a lot.

"I decided he was my real father. That Marga was only some kind of hired nurse. Eventually, of course, they took me away from Marga altogether; and then Max *was* my father, or the nearest thing.

"I trusted him.

"That was a mistake."

———

Susan said, "Why did they take you away from Marga?"

"She came home from the Safeway one morning and found me taking apart the radio. I was doing a pretty good job of it. I had it sorted by component size—quarter-watt resistors on the left, power supply on the right. Desoldered the parts with a needle from her sewing kit—I heated it over a candle. Burned myself a couple of times, but I was beginning to make sense of it."

"Marga was angry?"

"Marga was frightened, I think, *and* angry, and she was wearing The Look—which is really a kind of horror. Changeling in the crib, worm in the cornmeal . . ."

"She punished you," Susan guessed.

"She turned on the left-front burner on the Hotpoint and held my hand over it. Second-degree burns. I healed up pretty fast. But they took me away from her—or vice versa."

———

It wasn't all bad (John explained). There was more luxury than torture. He was pampered, really. And in some ways, it was an ordinary childhood. He had toys to play with. He remembered the extraordinary vividness of colors and sensations . . . the radiant blue luster of a crib toy, the pale intricate pastels of a sun-faded beachball; he remembered the letters etched on glass storefronts like black cuneiform ("chicken-tracks," Max called them), pleasing but mysterious.

He remembered the day he learned to read—acquiring the phonetics and the approximations of written English, puzzling out a newspaper headline to himself. He remembered riding into town on some errand with Dr. Kyriakides, and his amazement that the angular marks on signs and windows had resolved suddenly into *words*—A&P, USED BOOKS, WOOLWORTHS—this pleasure mixed with frustration because, having recognized the words, he could no longer see the lovely strange chicken-tracks. The marks had turned into words and words they stubbornly remained. The abstraction had displaced the concrete. Story of his life.

One by one, category by category, the objects of his perception faded into language. A tree became "tree"; "tree" became "a noun." Categorical hierarchies exploded around him, somehow more organic than the organic things they named. For instance, the oak in front of Marga's town house: even when he tried to focus exclusively on the texture of its bark or the color of its leaves, he triggered a network of associative ideas—gymnosperm and angiosperm, xylem and cambium, seed and fruit—that displaced the thing itself. He became afraid that his vision—that the world itself—might dissolve into a manic crystal-growth of pattern and symbol.

"It's an inevitable process," Max told him. "It's good. Nothing is lost."

John wondered whether this was true.

He began to understand the way in which he was different, though no one would really explain it and even Dr. Kyriakides dodged the subject. He learned how to slip into the research unit's small medical library when his keepers weren't looking, usually during lunch hours or bathroom breaks. The neurological tomes that resided there were too advanced for him, but he could divine a little of their subject. The brain. The mind. Intelligence.

On his fifth birthday he asked Dr. Kyriakides, "Did you make me the way I am?"

After a hesitation and a frown, Max admitted it. "Yes."

"Then you're my father."

"I suppose . . . in a way. But Marga wouldn't understand, if you told her."

"I won't tell her, then," John said.

It didn't matter. He understood.

Outside this small room in Toronto, the snow continued to fall. Susan wondered whether Amelie could see the snow. Whether Amelie was cold—wherever she was.

The tape recorder popped up a cassette. Susan inserted a new one.

"I trusted Max until he farmed me out to the Woodwards," John said. "Even then—at first—I gave him the benefit of the doubt."

The explanation was plain enough. Max had explained meticulously. The research was funded by the government and now the funding had been revoked. The legality of it was questionable and people were afraid of the truth getting out. John would have to be careful about what he told the Woodwards. "Also, we won't be able to see each other for a while. I hope you understand."

John didn't answer.

Max had checked the family out and they were decent enough people, an older couple, childless, referred through a contact in an adoption agency. "Obviously, they don't know what you are. You may have to conceal your nature. Do you understand? You'll have to become at least passably 'normal'—for everyone's sake."

John listened politely, watching Max across the barrier of his polished oak desk in this indifferent room, his book-lined office. "You have to do what the government tells you," he said to Max. John was five years old.

"Yes, I do. In this case."

"But you're a Communist," John said.

Max rose slightly in his chair. "What do you mean? Who told you that?"

"Nobody told me. I watch you when people talk about politics. I watched you when Kennedy came on TV and talked about Castro. Your face. Your eyes."

Max laughed. John was pleased: even at this terrible moment, the hour of his exile, he was able to make Max happy. "I should never mistake you for a child," Max said. "But I always do. No, I'm not a Communist. I was at one time. During the war. I gave it up when I came to this country. My uncle died fighting for Veloukhiotis, and it was pointless—completely futile. Now we have the Generals. Is there any sense in that? I don't believe in revolution any more."

"But you believe in the rest of it," John pressed. "Marxism. Leninism."

He had read the entry under "Communism" in the Columbia Encyclopedia and these questions had been on his mind.

"Not even that," Max said, more soberly. "I gave it all up."

"You stopped believing in Marxism?"

"Do you really want to know?"

John nodded.

"I stopped believing in 'the people.' I'm an apostate from that central faith. Marx believed that mankind was perfectible through economics. But it's a childish idea. People talk about Stalinism, but Stalinism is only fascism with a different accent, and fascism is simply the politics of the monkey cage. The failure is here"—he thumped his chest—"in the mechanism of the cells. In our ontogeny. If you want to perfect mankind, that's where you begin."

"But you still believe in the perfectibility of mankind."

"Wouldn't you rather talk about the Woodwards? Your future?"

"I want to know," John said.

"Whether I believe in the perfectibility of mankind? I will tell you this: human beings are cowards and thieves and torturers.

That I believe. And yes, I believe the species can be improved. Why not? The only alternative is despair."

But there's a contradiction here, John wanted to say. How could you want to improve a thing when you despised it so entirely to begin with? What could you build out of that contempt? —especially if the contempt encompasses your own being?

But he didn't ask. Max was going on about the Woodwards, about school—"Don't trust anyone," he said. "Anyone might be your enemy."

It was a sweeping statement. *Including you?* John wondered. *Should I mistrust you, too? Is that what this is all about?*

But it was not a question he could bring himself to ask. He was not a child, Max was right; but neither was he old enough to endure the possibility that he might be fundamentally alone in the world.

––––––––––

Life with the Woodwards, then, began as a deception, a concealment, not always successful. But at least he understood the rules of the game. For years John chose to believe that Max would eventually come and get him. Even if they couldn't be together, Max was still his truest father; Max cared about him.

He banked this belief in the most private recesses of his mind; he never allowed the flame to flicker. But Max did not come. And on his twelfth birthday, after a perfunctory celebration with the Woodwards, John began to admit to himself that Max might never come.

So he broke a promise. He went looking for Max.

It was spring, and he rode a bus into the city through thawing snow-patches and muddy lots. He had packed a bag lunch, solemnly. He ate it sitting on a transit bench outside Marga's old house, a couple of blocks from the university. Did he want to see Marga? He wasn't sure. But no one entered or left the house. The shutters were closed and the siding had been painted eggshell blue. Maybe Marga had moved away.

He stood and walked through the raw spring air to the research complex, to Max's office there.

He opened the door and walked in. Max looked up, maybe expecting to see an undergraduate, frowning when he recognized John. Max was older than John remembered him, fashionably shaggier; he had grown his sideburns long.

His eyes widened and then narrowed. "You shouldn't have come here."

"It's good to see you, too."

"Don't be flippant. I could lose my tenure. People in this building have long memories." He frowned at his watch. "Meet me in the parking lot. I have a car there—a black Ford."

John left the building and waited twenty minutes in the pallid sunlight, shivering on the curb beside the automobile. Then Max came striding out and opened the passenger door for him. John climbed aboard. "I wanted to see you," John said. "I wanted to talk."

"It's dangerous for both of us."

"I understand. You don't want to lose your job."

"I don't want to lose my job, and I presume you don't want to be brought to the attention of any powerful interests. We're privileged to be an inactive file in someone's cabinet. I would like to keep it that way."

"I thought you might try to see me. At least try."

Max compressed his lips. "I've driven past the Woodwards' house from time to time. Once I saw you walking to school. I have a contact at the Board of Education; he's been forwarding your records—"

"But we haven't *talked.*"

"We're not allowed to talk."

"Revolutionary," John mocked.

"You know I'm not."

"But you're brave enough to bend your ethics from time to time. For instance, a little genetic manipulation."

"Neurological, not genetic. Your genes are perfectly ordinary, I'm afraid. Do you resent it—being what you are?"

John shrugged.

Max said, "I rescued you from mediocrity."

"You rescued me from the human race!"

"It amounts to the same thing."

"Jesus, Max, how pathetically unimaginative!"

His rage took him by surprise: it was a sudden huge pressure in his chest. He said, "I'm more than you ever dreamed of. I could kill us both, you know. It's been seven years. Things have changed. If I wanted you to you'd drive right off the retaining wall of this freeway. You don't believe it? But just think, Max. Think how nice it would be. Like flying. Flying out into the void. A little gas, a little twist of the wheel. Like *flying*, Max—"

The words had spilled out of him. He stopped, aware of the sweat beading on Max's brow, the way his fingers trembled on the wheel.

My God, he thought. It's true. I *could* do that.

He felt suddenly cold.

"You can drop me at the off ramp," he said.

Max pulled up obediently near a bus stop, wordless and wide-eyed. John climbed out without saying goodbye. He watched as the black Ford shuddered away from the curb and merged uncertainly with the traffic.

Twelve years old.

Alone on this empty, wide boulevard.

It was nighttime now, and very cold.

———

A week later, John retrieved the journals from Max's safe.

He told the Woodwards he was sleeping over at a friend's house. They were pleased to hear that he had finally made a friend and didn't press him for details. He took the night bus into town and waited until the research unit was locked and dark. Then he shinnied up a maple tree and through one of the high access windows, hinged open to moderate the fierce heating system.

He took the documents from the safe under Max's desk, photocopied them on the Xerox machine in the adjoining room, then returned the originals. He folded the copies and tucked them under his belt in order to keep his hands free.

In the corridor outside Max's office he was surprised by a security guard.

The guard was a fat bald man in a blue suit with a pistol at his hip. He came around an angle in the hallway and stood gawking at John for a long instant before dashing forward.

John discovered that he was calm, that he was able to return the guard's stare and stand his ground. He should have been frightened. Instead, he felt something else . . . a heady combination of power and contempt. Because the guard was transparent: every twitch betrayed his thoughts. He was a machine, John thought. A noisy engine of belligerence and fear.

He spoke up before the guard could find words, made his own voice calm and uninflected: "I want to leave. No one has to know I was here." Then watched the wheels turning as the imperatives registered, uncertainty turning down the corners of the man's mouth and narrowing his eyes. *If I phone this in I'll have to fill out a fucking report;* it was as good as reading his mind. "I ought to kick your ass," the guard began, but it was not so much a threat as a question: can I say this?

"Don't," John said.

The guard backed off a step.

Amazing. John knew about suggestibility and the phenomenon of hypnosis, but he was surprised at how *effortless* it was, how utterly pleasurable. He had bypassed all the barriers; he was talking now directly to the delicate core of self behind this uniform: he pictured something wet and pinkly quivering, an "ego." It was an easy target.

He said, "Open the door at the back."

The guard turned and led him down the hallway.

At the door the spell seemed to falter. "Thieving little bastard," the guard said. "I ought to—"

But John silenced him with a look.

He transferred the thick manila folder of photocopies from his belt to his hand. The guard was standing directly behind him, but didn't see—or didn't want to.

John closed the door and listened as the lock slid home.

The night air was cold and bracing. He stood for a moment in the shadow of a tree, smiling. He felt good. Felt *free*. Freer than he had ever been before.

Reading the research notes, he was shocked to find Marga described as "an unemployed, gravid white female of doubtful morals"—shocked in general by the tone of callous indifference Max had assumed. But he supposed Max had already cast his lot with Homo Superior. This was contempt by proxy, the exploitation of the old order for the sake of the new. Max did not believe in "the people." Presumably Marga was a thief and a torturer *manqué*.

The story of his genesis, however, the intrauterine injections and the forced cortical growth, made perfect sense. He had guessed much of this before.

In a way, the theft had been more revealing than the notes themselves. His commandeering of the security guard, his intimidation of Max a few days earlier, had forced a new discovery: *he was not weak*. He had allowed himself to be dominated by Max's fears, by the idea that he was different and therefore vulnerable. How intoxicating now to suspect that he might be more than a freak: that he might be *functionally* superior, better at the things human beings were good at.

A better hunter. A better predator.

"But you still cared about the Woodwards," Susan said.

Night had fallen. The window was dark, though the snow still beat against it. Susan switched on a lamp.

"I kept them separate in my mind," John admitted. "I made a special exception for James Woodward. He was an ordinary man and there was nothing I owed him. But I harbored fantasies about pleasing him."

"It mattered to you."

"It shouldn't have."

"But it did."

"I think—" He hesitated. "I think I just didn't want to be disappointed again."

———

They had missed lunch altogether, and now it was past dinnertime. Susan went down to the kitchen, fixed a couple of sandwiches and carried them upstairs.

After coffee, John switched on a portable radio for the weather forecast. The news wasn't good. Record snowfall, schools closed until further notice, City Hall begging motorists to stay off the roads. John shook his head. "We can't wait much longer."

To find Amelie, he meant. As if it would be that simple.

But Susan sensed the urgency in his voice.

"No more talk," he said.

The streetlights were a distant blur through the snow-crusted windows. A gust of wind rattled the panes, and Susan stood up to go to her room.

John reached for her hand.

She hesitated.

"Stay," he said. "Please stay."

It was a request, Susan thought. It was not a compulsion, not a demand. She could have left.

She didn't.

20

It was his life. But not all his life.

He lay beside her in the darkness and wondered whether his sudden surfeit of conscience was actually Benjamin's: a wisp of that other self. The touch of Susan's skin against him was a rebuke, almost painful. She was asleep. He moved against her. She was warm and there was snow against the ice-laced window. He had gone cotton-mouthed laboring at the day's intimacy, an intimacy of words; honest as far as it went . . . but oblique, polished, limited.

He hadn't told her, for instance, about that first act of seduction, the act that had haunted him ever since—most recently in a motel room in Alberta. Seduction as bestiality—making love to the Look. Skin fucking skin, souls in absentia. The story of his life. Except for tonight, with Susan; tonight had been different.

But if this was Benjamin's conscience that had begun to prick him, then here was an even more disturbing notion: maybe it was Benjamin who had allowed him this moment just past. Maybe it was Benjamin who had maneuvered around the Look; maybe it was Benjamin's sincerity she had registered—Benjamin's eyes she had looked into.

Maybe, all those years ago, when he bullied a girl into his bed for the first time, maybe it was Benjamin or some proto-Benjamin or shadow Benjamin who had roused from sleep and pronounced the traitorous words "I love you," uncalled-for and unwanted, a tacit admission of absurdity, utterly unallowable.

Benjamin, not John, who provoked love. Benjamin who loved Amelie and was loved by Amelie. Benjamin the idiot, *savant* only in the mathematics of this fathomless emotion.

God damn you, he thought, you truncated false and stupid thing. You prosthetic imitation of a human being.

God damn you for succeeding at it.

———

A surfeit of conscience and a memory he could not suppress: this does not make for easy sleep.

He listened awhile to the beat of the snow against the window.

After a time, without thinking, he reached up and brushed away Susan's hair from her ear. The ear was a pink, shadowy cusp in the darkness. He moved his lips, experimentally—hardly more than a whisper.

"I love you," he said.

She didn't stir.

But he was calmer now, and slept.

PART III
UNCONTROLLED EXPERIMENTS

21

In the morning Susan re-packed her luggage (most of it untouched since her return from California) and went looking for Dr. Kyriakides.

She found him in the study. He was bent over his desk, making notes in a loose-leaf binder. He looked up when she opened the door. How old he seems, Susan thought—suddenly old and humorless.

"We're leaving today," she said. "John and I. We're going to find Amelie."

Dr. Kyriakides did not react at once. Slowly, he peeled away his glasses and massaged the bridge of his nose. The silence was professorial, devastating; Susan wanted to cringe.

He said, "That's absurd."

"You can't stop us."

"Of course I can't. You're both adults. You can do what you like. But surely you must see—well, for one thing, Susan, consider the weather! You'd be lucky to get a mile down the road. And I'm certain neither of you know where to find Amelie, wherever she might be. We can't even be certain she wants to be found. All we know is that she left the house without warning last Saturday— which is her privilege, as it is yours." He shook his head. "It might be understandable that John conceived this idea. He's ill, after all. He has a neurological illness. But you, Susan! I thought you were interested in his welfare! Not coddling his disease."

In spite of herself, Susan blushed. "That's *not* what I'm doing. John is perfectly lucid."

"It was his idea?"

"Yes."

"Doesn't it seem a little out of character?"

"I don't know what you mean."

"He has no interest in Amelie! It was *Benjamin* who cared about her. John is as far beyond Amelie Desjardins as we are advanced beyond the starfish. And you know it. Why would he want to risk his life for her? Because that's what this would mean, after all. He seems fine, but the crisis could come at any moment. Fever and disorientation and possibly unconsciousness—possibly death. Can you cope with that? Do you want that to happen while your car is buried in a snowdrift miles from here?"

"It's important to him."

"Is it? Has he told you why? Or is this your own conclusion?"

Susan shook her head. "I don't want to have this discussion. I just thought you should know we're leaving."

She turned away.

"Wait," Dr. Kyriakides said, and Susan was embarrassed to discover she could not resist the command.

She hesitated at the doorway.

"John talked about me—didn't he? That's what this is all about."

"He talked about himself," Susan said.

"You know I never meant this to happen."

His voice was suddenly chastened and tentative. He stood up, stepped out from behind the desk. *He's a small man,* Susan thought. *He's shorter than I am.* Another brand-new observation.

"I had no idea things would turn out the way they did. At every step—please try to understand—I made what I thought was the best decision. The wisest decision. Even when I was tampering with John *in utero,* even when I was dealing with his mother. She was a stupid woman, Susan. She would have had a stupid child and they would have lived stupid, ordinary lives. She was the kind of passive and amoral creature that allowed a Hitler to come to power—a Stalin." The words were fervent and his expression was utterly sincere; Susan was transfixed. "When I created John," he said, "I meant to break that chain. I was funded by a mercenary organization for a mercenary purpose, it's true, but I never believed the government would benefit from my work in any substantial way. If anything, the opposite. I meant to create a better human being, for whom they would therefore have no use. Not just 'more intelligent' in the obvious sense. Authentically better." He shook his head. "But it's a terrible burden, and I should not have imposed it on John. I understand that now. I—"

"God damn your pious self-pity!"

She had not planned to say this; the words came spilling out. Her fists were clenched and her fingernails bit into her palms. Dr. Kyriakides gaped at her. "That's all we are to you—all of us—just stupid, ordinary people! You took a child and you fed him all that contempt, that arrogance! Christ, of *course* it was a burden! Isn't it obvious? That's why he had to invent Benjamin." She turned away. No more hesitation. "That's why we have to leave."

———

She was too shaken to drive. John slid behind the wheel of the Honda. He had excavated the car from a mound of snow, but the driveway was still solid—Susan wondered whether they would get as far as the road.

But she put her faith in John and curled up into the private space of her winter coat. The snow tires whined and finally bit against the blacktop; the Honda struggled forward.

According to the radio, the snow might begin again tonight. A second front was pushing in from the high prairies. But for now the sky was a glassy, vacant blue, cold and clear. Susan scrubbed frost from the window next to her and peered out at a frigid rural landscape of frozen ponds and hydroelectric clearances. The highway had been ploughed during the night, but a morning wind had scattered snow back across the tarmac in serpentine dunes.

Now the Honda picked up speed. It occurred to Susan that John was driving too fast for the road—but she looked at him and was reassured. His eyes had taken on an intense, powerful focus; his touch on the wheel was delicate and certain.

The road sped away behind them. Susan was warm and calmer now; she sat up and stretched.

"You told Max we were leaving?"

She nodded. "He says it's pointless. He says you don't know how to find Amelie."

"I don't, precisely. I think I know where to begin."

"You don't really know that much about her, do you?"

"No."

"But Benjamin does."

He nodded.

"And you have access to that," Susan said. "To his memories—his life."

"More than I used to. That makes it easier. But even Benjamin didn't know all about Amelie."

"She told me about her brother," Susan said. "He tried to kidnap her the day she moved. You think he's involved in this?"

"That would be an obvious suspicion. Nothing is certain, of course. All we really know is that she left without leaving a message."

"Maybe she just got tired of us all."

"That's possible."

"But you don't believe it."

"No," he said. "I don't believe it."

They crossed the city limits. Coming down Yonge Street, John slowed to deal with traffic. Susan watched a TTC bus slide into an intersection, its wheels locked. A pickup truck swerved to avoid it; John pumped the brake and kept the Honda a carlength back. A brisk wind peppered the windshield with crystals of yesterday's snow, glittering in the sunlight.

They were well into the city when Susan felt the Honda's motion grow more erratic; she heard John catch his breath as they fishtailed coming around a curve. Just north of Eglinton he pulled into a parking lot. "Can you drive us the rest of the way? It shouldn't be too hard. The roads have been cleared since morning."

He was sweating. Susan frowned. "Are you all right?"

John held up his hand to show her the tremor, which was obvious and pronounced.

Oh, God, Susan thought.

"I think we'd be safer," John said calmly, "if you took over for a while."

————

There was this to deal with, too: his "change."

They rented a room at a downtown hotel not far from Yonge Street. They unpacked the few things they had brought, including the Woodward guitar Susan had carried back from Chicago. Meager fractions of their lives. She rested on the bed while John showered.

"The change" was something she didn't really want to think about. Dr. Kyriakides had intimated that John might die. John said that wasn't really likely . . . but the question was open. And there was nothing that Susan or anyone else could do about it: no real treatment apart from the bottle of pills Dr. Collingwood had prescribed. There were questions she would have to begin to face, unpleasant as they were, such as: What would happen if John collapsed? Should she take him to a hospital?

This was all beyond her.

For now she was simply accommodating John's wishes, helping him find Amelie. After that . . . well, it was impossible to predict. She remembered Dr. Kyriakides describing John's illness as "a radical neurological retrenchment, a shedding of the induced growth . . . a one-time event, which he might survive in one form or another."

One form or another. As John or Benjamin. Or some unpredictable amalgamation of the two.

And the event would be traumatic, Dr. Kyriakides had said: like a fever, it would run its course, would peak, would then be finished and its effects irrevocable.

He'll be different, Susan thought. He'll want me with him. Or he won't. He won't be the same: something new will have been born . . . something will have died.

But now he is John, she told herself sternly. The future was always the future, always mysterious. What mattered was that he was John and she was with him now.

———

He came out of the shower looking stronger, though there was a certain persistent hollowness about his eyes that Susan didn't like.

"It's early," he said. "We haven't had lunch. Let's head over to Yonge Street—the place Amelie used to work."

They braved the cutting wind. Susan was afraid the Goodtime wouldn't be open; a lot of places had closed because of the weather. But the lights were all on and the sign in the window said, OPEN REGULAR HOURS.

Their waitress was a tiny, timid-looking woman named Tracy; the food was greasy but filling. When Tracy came back with their coffee, John asked about Amelie.

Tracy gave him a wide-eyed stare. "I don't know anything, anything about that!"

She hurried off with the check still clutched in her hand.

John looked at Susan. Susan shrugged.

It was the manager who brought back the check. He wiped his hands on his apron and said, "What's this about Amelie?"

"She's missing," John said. "We're looking for her."

"So? She's not here."

"I know that. I thought she might have talked to somebody."

"Haven't seen her. Haven't talked to her."

"Well, all right." John stood up. "Your waitress—Tracy—she seemed pretty nervous."

The manager began an answer, then hesitated and took a closer look at John. John returned it steadily. Susan wondered if this was John's "hypnotic" power at work, though she could see no sign of it—saw instead maybe a calculated sincerity.

Then the manager seemed to reach a decision. "There was somebody else here asking after Amelie. Tracy's just skittish . . . she gets upset."

"Somebody else?"

"Her brother, Tracy says. Big guy. Kind of strange. But he hasn't been back for a while."

———

Susan said, "It only confirms what we suspected."

"But that's important," John said. "That's useful."

He led her back through the snowy streets—not to the hotel, but to the doughnut shop on Wellesley where she had discovered him all those months ago. Susan wondered if this was some kind of deliberate irony . . . but John was too serious for that. He took the table with the chessboard engraved on its surface; Susan sat opposite him. "What now?"

"We sit here for a while. Carbohydrates and coffee. We look around."

"What are we looking for?"

"I don't know yet." He shrugged out of his jacket. "You want a game?"

"Won't that be distracting?"

"No."

"All right, then."

They played twice. The first game was a rout. Susan's mind wasn't focused on the board—she was cold, and frightened by what the manager at the Goodtime had said—and John pried out her castled king with a bishop sacrifice; checkmate came quickly.

She took the second game more seriously. She played a King's Indian defense and pondered each move scrupulously. By playing a combination of aggressive and defensive moves she was able to keep him at arm's length. Her interest deepened. She saw a chance to open up his king—a knight fork that would force a pawn move; she would lose the knight, but it would leave her bishop and her queen in a single, powerful diagonal aimed at his broken pawn ranks. Was there a flaw in this reasoning? Well, probably . . . but Susan couldn't find it. She shrugged and advanced the knight.

John captured it with his pawn.

Susan hunched down over the board. If she brought the bishop down—and then the queen, while his knight was still pinned—

John said, "Look."

She raised her head.

A man had just come through the door. A short man in a heavy coat, shivering. He bought a doughnut and coffee at the counter, turned and spotted John.

Recognition flashed between them. The man muttered and turned toward the door.

Susan whispered, *"Who is he?"*

"His name is Tony Morriseau," John said, "and we need to talk to him."

She stood up with John and cast a last glance at the chessboard. She was a move away from checkmate. He hadn't noticed.

———

Chess, John had told her, was mainly a memory trick. The difference between a chess master and a "civilian" player was that the master had stored a vast internal library of potential positions and was able to recognize them as they developed on the board. That, plus a certain finely honed ability to concentrate attention, made all the difference.

John was not technically a master because he had not played in enough tournaments to acquire a significant rating. His chess playing had been an amusement. ("An experiment," he once called it.) He had played, at least in those days, to relish his easy superiority over his competitors. It was a cruel, private entertainment. Or so he claimed. But Susan remembered what he had said when they first met, across this table, when she asked why he went on playing when it was obvious that he would win: *"One hopes,"* he had said.

Hopes for an equal, she thought. Hopes for recognition, for understanding. Hopes for a touch, for a contact, miraculously, across that divide.

What matters, Susan thought, is that he had never really abandoned that hope. Even now, deep in this killing winter. It was alive inside him.

She took a last look at the chessboard, then followed him toward the door.

22

John followed Tony Morriseau out into the cold afternoon.

A bank of snowclouds had rolled in from the west; the sunlight was fading into winter dusk. Strange how vivid all this seemed. It was true, what he had told Susan: since childhood he had lived in a world of Platonic abstraction. Schema and essence, the word behind the shadow. It was Benjamin who had inhabited the universe of surfaces and colors.

But that was changing. He felt it now, and he felt it accelerating. He stepped into the biting winter air in a shower of snow crystals, and he was stunned by the immediacy of it all. Was this how Susan experienced things? All sense and no *cogitans*—this playground of perception? Made it hard to think.

He was deluged by dusk and snowdunes, by the amber glow of the streetlights so cold and melancholy they seemed to burn into his sight. The knife of the wind. The hiss of his breath.

How *meaningful* it all seemed: a new and ancient language . . .

"John?"

Susan's voice was crystalline and intimate. He turned to look at her. She was beautiful. She was frowning. "Are you all right?"

He shook his head. Maybe he wasn't. He started to say, "I—" But the word itself hovered in the air, a pure and absurd syllable. It had no antecedent. He was as hollow as the sky.

Please, not now, he thought.

"Just a little dizzy," he said.

"He turned the corner south of here," Susan said.

John hurried after the retreating figure of Tony Morriseau, forcing recollection on himself. Tony Morriseau who had sold him the Corvette . . . Tony Morriseau the drug dealer, who might know something about Amelie.

Amelie whom he must find, because he had assigned himself this task. For Benjamin, it was the repayment of a debt. For John . . . say, an experiment with an idea. An idea about lineage. An idea about descent.

Tony was too proud to run and John caught up with him in the blank whiteness of a parking lot, the streetlights splaying out weird shadows all around them. Tony whirled and said, "Fuck off!"

"We need to talk," John said. He heard Susan behind him now: her cold breath and the squeal of her boots against the snow.

"We don't have anything to talk about," Tony said.

"About Roch. About Amelie."

"I don't know anything about them."

But Tony was lying. John heard it in the angle of his words, brittle phonemes like tiny shards of ice. Tony knew Roch and Amelie from their street days: John remembered Amelie talking about it. "Tell the truth," John said.

"Go fuck yourself," Tony said.

But John possessed the key to Tony's soul. Tony was a small, pale, undefended thing under his shell of skin and it was not difficult to trick him out. He had done it before. "You talked to Roch."

Tony looked suddenly doubtful. "Yes . . ."

"What did he want?"

But now Tony frowned and canted his head. "Why should I tell you?"

And John was startled.

"Because—" he began.

But the words weren't there.

They had always been there before.

"Asshole," Tony said.

Susan stepped forward. She looked small and delicate in the snow. "Please," she said.

Tony shifted to look at her.

"Amelie's in trouble," Susan went on. "If you know Roch, you know the kind of trouble I mean. All we want is to find her."

"What are you, her social worker?"

"Her friend."

"I talked to Roch," Tony said, "but not about Amelie."

"He bought something from you?"

"Not from me. A guy I know. What he wanted, I don't have. All right? That's it, that's all I have to say."

John collected himself. "Did he tell you where he was going?"

Tony regarded him with instant contempt; he began to speak, then hesitated. John was connecting, but only sporadically. "No," Tony said. "Except—he mentioned something about 'the warehouse.' He said he was 'going to sleep in the fucking warehouse tonight.' That was last week. I don't know what it means." Tony frowned massively. "Just get the hell away from me, all right? I would really appreciate that."

He turned and was gone across the parking lot toward the lights on Yonge Street.

———

John was suddenly dizzy. Susan put a steadying arm around him.

"John? Can you make it back to the hotel?"

He felt her warm presence against the cold dark and decided he could.

23

Susan wrapped her arm around John's waist and helped him through the hotel lobby, ignoring the hostile stare of the desk clerk; maneuvered him up the elevator and through the door of the room. He was cooperative but loose-jointed; his body radiated a feverish heat.

She stretched him out across the bed. "John? Can you hear me?"

He turned his face toward her. His eyes were glazed but attentive. He nodded.

She put her hand across his forehead and drew it quickly back. The fever was intense and Susan felt a surge of panic. She couldn't deal with this! She wasn't trained for it! He needed a doctor, a hospital—

He reached up suddenly and took her wrist in a clamping grip.

"I need aspirin," he said. "Maybe cold compresses. This will pass."

She nodded until her agreement registered and his hand slipped away.

She undressed him and pulled blankets over him, then hurried down to the hotel's convenience shop for a bottle of Bayer's. When she got back, he was shivering and moaning. She fed him three tablets with a glass of tap water and pulled up a chair by the bedside.

———

The snow that had been predicted all day had settled in by nine o'clock. Susan watched it through the hotel window. It was a picturesque, gentle, persistent snowfall; the big flakes danced against the window and drifted onto the ledge outside. The snow obscured the city lights and softened the murmur of the traffic.

With the snowfall, John's fever began to retreat.

Susan pressed a damp washcloth against his forehead. He had been sleeping restlessly for the last two hours; it was only forty-five minutes since the fever had broken and his temperature had dropped back to normal. He needs the rest, Susan thought. But when she took the cloth away, he sat up.

"I did what you told me," Susan said.

"You did fine."

"Are you better now?"

"Better than I was a little while ago."

"Is this it?" Susan asked. "Is this what Dr. Kyriakides said would happen?"

"Let's not talk about it now."

———

She took a shower. She immersed herself in the hot rush of the water. Washing away the fear, she thought. Washing away today and washing away tomorrow.

She wrapped herself in a towel and entered the darkened bedroom. John was propped up in the bed, a faint silhouette. Susan toweled her shoulders a last time, then climbed in beside him.

The bed was hot and faintly damp. A sickroom bed. She didn't care. His body was warm, but it was an ordinary warmth now. Because she was afraid, Susan pressed herself against him; he turned to face her.

"This might happen again," she guessed.

He nodded. She felt the motion against her cheek.

"Might be worse the next time?"

"It might be."

She absorbed this information.

She said, "Did it mean anything to you, what that man said about 'the warehouse?' "

"It's an empty building down by the lakeshore—Amelie told me about it. He might have taken her there. We'll go tomorrow and have a look."

"In the snow?"

"In the snow. I'll be all right."

———

The snow fell steadily far into the night. Susan heard it tapping against the pane of the window. Begging admittance, she thought. But it can't come in.

Neither of them slept. The silence was a vast tapestry, stitched with the sound of their voices.

"Why me?" Susan asked. "Why did you choose me?"

To be with him in this bed, she meant. To touch him in the darkness.

He said, "Because we're alike."

"Are we?"

"In a way."

"What way?"

"Because both of us have lost something. A certain kind of connection."

"I don't understand." The wind rattled the window.

"We're orphans," he said. "Isn't that obvious? We're feral children. We don't know how to be human." He touched her cheek. "That's what we have in common."

Susan was too sleepy to explore this in all its nuances.

She said, "What we have in common is what we *don't* have."

"Yes."

"A father."

"Lineage," John said. "Ancestry."

"A father," Susan confirmed. In the tranquility of the snow-bound darkness she was able to admit it. She had been looking for a father ever since her father died; she had found a sort of father —at least temporarily—in Dr. Kyriakides.

She was embarrassed to realize she had said this out loud.

"But you want more than that," John said. "Something finer and better."

She nodded.

He said, "You would have slept with him—if he'd asked."

"Yes. I guess I would have. I almost did. Isn't that strange? There was one time . . . he took me to dinner . . . but he said he's not interested in women. In men, once, but even that was a long time ago." She rolled over and felt John's hand slide up her shoulder. "He's not a good man, is he? But still . . . at least he's been able to help you."

"No," John said. "I'm sorry, Susan. No, he hasn't."

"Not cure you. But he said he gave you a prescription—"

"He gave me dopamine. It's what they give Alzheimer's patients. In my case, it's not much more than a placebo." Susan turned to face him. He smiled in the dark. "Max can't do anything to help me. He never could. That's not why he came looking for me."

"Why, then?"

"Guilt," John said. "Remorse. And to finish the experiment."

———

Later, he said he was thirsty. Susan brought him a glass of water from the bathroom tap. He sipped it in the dark.

She said, "Do you know everything about me?"

"Yes," he said solemnly. "And you know everything about me."

———

But not really. Not everything.

Curled against him, she whispered: "Will you die?"

She strained to hear his answer against the hissing of the wind.

"I don't know," he said finally. "I've thought about it. What's happening to me is very powerful, a powerful process. I feel it. It's like an engine running inside me. Very strong. It's not something you can simply resist. You have to bend—this way or that. But that's the hard part. Even if I can bargain with it, I'm not sure . . . I don't know if it's a deal I want to make."

He held her against him; but Susan was wordless in the dark, and this time the silence lingered.

24

Amelie knew where her brother had taken her: it was the place they called "the warehouse."

At least, she and Roch had called it that. It wasn't really a warehouse. It was a big abandoned building beside the railway tracks, where the CPR line ran along the lakeshore west of the city. Many years ago, Roch once told her, the building had contained a fur-storage business. Now it was a cold, dark warren of cavernous rooms and windowless chambers. And she was confined in it.

She remembered how she had come here—but dimly, dimly.

She had gone into the city to meet her mother, but it turned out that there was no bus from Montreal scheduled at that hour. So she had milled around through the crowded, oppressively hot terminal for almost an hour . . . and then Roch put his hand on her shoulder, and she *knew* it was Roch, knew it instinctively and immediately. He took her arm. She wanted to break free but couldn't. He led her out to his van and then he locked her in the back.

They drove to a vacant lot by the CPR line and Roch parked and climbed in back with her. He had something in his hand: a syringe—

Memory clouded. But she remembered him carrying her through the snow at dusk, his strong arms enfolding her. She had recognized the way to the warehouse, where they used to go when there was nowhere else to sleep. But only in summer. It was winter now, and cold, and the snow was deep and getting deeper. Someone will see us, she thought. The railroad police will see us for sure. But the railroad police, who sometimes parked along these tracks, weren't here now. The snow was too deep and recent. Everybody had gone home. Everybody had found a warm place to stay.

The warehouse . . .

The property had been in litigation for years. It was worthless. Someday the building would be torn down. For now, it was abandoned and dangerous. Even when they came here during their time on the street, Amelie would never venture very far inside. There were bats living in the old cold-storage chambers; there were drippy, ancient pipes and wild raccoons and bad smells. Since then, apparently, Roch had explored the building. He had a big Eveready flashlight in one hand, and he pulled Amelie stumbling after him with the other. There were rooms and corridors so deep inside this building that no light penetrated from the outside; cracked linoleum or bare concrete floors drifted with sawdust and animal droppings. Roch put her over his shoulder, took the handle of the flashlight in his teeth, and climbed a narrow wooden ladder to a higher, darker level. In a small room here at the heart of the building, he dumped her against the chipped plaster wall and started a small Sterno fire. The smoke wafted up to the ceiling and dissipated through a hole there, up and up in lazy curls. The room did not warm appreciably.

Amelie was a spectator to all this. She felt abstracted from her body. What had Roch put into her? A drug, she thought. Something lazy, distancing, and slightly nauseating. She lifted her hand and looked at it: it seemed to be floating in midair.

She watched Roch pace the room, checking the entrance and fiddling with the Sterno. There was a question she wanted to ask. It was on the tip of her tongue. She worked hard to recall it.

"Roch . . . what is it you want? What do you want from me?"

He turned his face toward her, but only briefly. His eyes were blank with indifference. He stood up briskly.

"This isn't about you," he said. "You don't matter anymore."

25

The snow had paralyzed the city. Overnight, a winter blizzard had accumulated drifts and depths that the snowplows could not shunt aside, at least not quickly or efficiently. The main arteries were reduced to a single lane; the subways were running but the buses were not. Susan awoke to an absolute silence: the traffic outside the hotel had been utterly stilled.

John was in the bathroom—she could hear the shower running.

She went to the window. Outside, the streets were transformed. The city was white, unsullied, and motionless. The snow had stopped falling but the sky was a uniform grey.

Good, she thought. We can't go anywhere today. It wasn't a blizzard; it was a reprieve.

She turned when she heard the water stop. John appeared at the bathroom door in his Levis: skinny, pale, a little shaky . . . but his eyes were bright and lucid.

"Get dressed," he said. "We don't have time to waste."

I should have expected this, Susan thought. There *was* no reprieve. It wasn't possible.

He couldn't afford one. He didn't have the time.

"It's an old building down by the lakeshore," John said over breakfast. "Amelie showed me one time when we were out walking."

Susan hesitated over her eggs. "Showed *you?*"

He was momentarily puzzled. "Showed Benjamin, I mean."

"An abandoned building," Susan repeated. "You think Amelie's there—Roch took her there?"

"I'm almost certain of it."

"Is it safe to go there?"

"No. It's not safe at all."

"We could call the police," Susan said. "We don't even have to tell them about Roch. Say we spotted some vagrants on the premises."

John shook his head. "Maybe that would flush him out. But I think, if he were cornered, he might just kill her. It's pointless, but it's the kind of gesture Roch might make."

"How can you know that? You never met him."

"I met him once," John corrected her.

"And you know that about him?"

"I know that about him."

"You're just going to walk in and take her away from him?"

"If I can."

"Maybe he *wants* you to come. Maybe he's jealous, he's out there waiting for you . . . that's why he told Tony Morriseau where he was going."

"Maybe," John admitted.

"How can you just walk into that?"

"Because I have to. It's a debt. I want to pay it off. Not just a debt to Amelie." He regarded Susan solemnly across the table. "I'll tell you another secret. There are lives I could have saved.

Thousands, maybe even hundreds of thousands. But I didn't. So I have to save *this* life, Amelie's life. It's not just one more experiment, Susan. It's the only experiment that matters."

She didn't know what he meant, but it was impossible to ask—there was a ferocity under the words that she was afraid to provoke.

He stood up suddenly, put down money for the bill. "The roads should be clear by now," he said.

———

They stopped at a Home Hardware outlet off Yonge Street, miraculously open for business although there was only one clerk inside. John bought a heavy-duty flashlight and fresh batteries and assembled them as Susan drove south and west through the snowbound streets.

She followed his directions toward the lakeshore west of the city, over the railroad tracks and into a labyrinth of warehouses and crumbling brick factories where the snow lay in pristine mountains and the little Honda labored like a crippled pack-mule. She parked when he told her to park. The silence was sudden and absolute. "We walk from here," he said.

Susan was dressed in high boots, a ski jacket, jeans. She tore the jacket sleeve while climbing through a hole in the fence that defined the railroad right-of-way. Now we're trespassing, she thought. Now the police will come and arrest us. But there were no police; there was only the snow clinging to the tree branches and the soft sound it made when it fell; the glitter of the tracks where an early morning train had polished the rails.

She followed John along the arc of the railway for a hundred yards or more, then scrambled after him up an embankment.

"There," he said. "That's the building."

Susan stood panting and looked up.

The building was huge. It was an old black brick building on an abandoned railway siding, sooty and Victorian. There were no windows, but the open loading bay gaped like a toothless mouth.

The snow had not softened or warmed this building, Susan thought. It was big and indifferent and it frightened her.

John's gaze was fixed on it. "I want you to stay here," he said. "If I bring Amelie out, help me get her to the car. Give me twenty minutes inside. If I'm not out by then, find a phone and call the police. Understand?"

"Yes." She looked at him critically. "John? Are you sure—I mean, are you all right?"

He shrugged.

"For now," he said.

She watched him walk away from her, toward the building; and she understood with a sudden, aching finality that she had been afraid of this place all along, even before she knew it existed—this dark chamber where he was determined to go—and that she could not stop him or bring him back.

26

Roch was pretty comfortable in the warehouse.

Sure, it was cold. Of course. But the Sterno fire helped. More important, he was alone here . . . except for Amelie, and he was able to keep Amelie sufficiently blissed out that she was not a real presence.

He was alone in this vast, empty building and it occurred to him that this was his natural state; that he had discovered his ideal habitat. His problems had always been with other people—their prudishness and their nasty glances. He was a stranger out there in the world. What he needed was what he had found: his own kingdom, *this* place. He moved down these dark and windowless corridors with the flashlight in his hand, king of the lightbeams, his pockets stuffed with a treasury of D batteries, and when he laughed his breath smoked out in front of him.

Of course, he had a purpose here. None of this was random motion. He was waiting for the man Amelie used to live with. No, more than that. He was waiting for justice.

He had left a trail and he believed the man would follow it. If not, maybe Roch would wheedle an address or a phone number from Amelie—she was cooperative, in her present condition—and the challenge could be issued more formally. But it would be better simply to lure the man here. "Benjamin," Amelie had said his name was. (She whispered it to the air from time to time.) But the name didn't matter. What mattered was the humiliation Roch had suffered in Amelie's apartment, months ago, and its sequel, his humiliation at Cherry Beach, both events now blurring into a long history of similar humiliations for which they had become emblematic. Roch understood that his life was an arrow, with moment following moment like the points of a trajectory toward some target not wholly of his own choosing. But he was happy in that service and he was happy to have found a home here.

He explored the snowbound building in great detail. He avoided the ground level, where there had been extensive vandalism and where the walls were emblazoned with vulgar graffiti. He preferred the lightless upper regions, closed to the world, a wooden ladder and the Eveready flashlight his admittance into a pure and angular wilderness. He also liked the cold-storage chambers at the rear, where the furs used to hang behind the loading bays, though these were less hospitable: bleak caverns where snowmelt dripped from corroded freon pipes and animal dung lay thick on the floor.

Time was nearly meaningless here . . . or would have been, save for the periodic demands of his body and the ticking clock of Amelie. Now he ambled past a shuttered window where rags of winter light penetrated from the west. Afternoon, therefore. He circled back to the room where Amelie, bound at the ankles, had crawled closer to the Sterno fire, some instinct for warmth operating through the narcotic haze. She seemed to be asleep; her breathing was shallow and periodic. Roch considered giving her another injection, then decided not to. It would be too easy to kill

her. This was a ticklish business. Still . . . even if he *did* kill her
. . . hadn't she served her purpose already? Assuming "Benjamin" showed up. She was disposable, really, except as a potential
hostage against some emergency Roch could not entirely frame or
predict. Dead, she would only have to be disposed of.

Still—

But he hesitated in his deliberation, startled to a new level of
alertness by the distant but distinct sound of footsteps in the
cavernous space of the warehouse.

It was a cue. He recognized it. Time had resumed its forward
march. His heart began to batter against his ribs.

He picked up a fifteen-inch copper pipe segment he had set
aside in rehearsal for this moment. A weapon in one hand, the
Eveready flashlight in the other. Be prepared. The Boy Scout's
Motto, ha-ha.

A smile formed on his lips.

27

Passing into the shadow of the building, John felt its presence as a physical chill.

He didn't know this building, but Amelie had told him about it. (Told him, told Benjamin: in memory the merger was already complete.) It was a huge, cold, black-brick nautilus shell and she hated it. He understood why.

But that was pathology, John thought, his sense of the building's soullessness. Because buildings don't have souls, ever. He had read extensively in abnormal psychology, not psychoanalytic case histories but the infinitely subtler literature of brain dysfunction. And it struck him that what he felt now was like the "heightened significance" in the intrarictal consciousness of temporal lobe epileptics. The limbic system bleeding into perception . . . animal foreboding injected into the loom and bulk of this stony Victorian structure. But then, he knew what might be inside.

He took a step up onto the ancient loading bay. The wooden platform creaked ominously. He could smell the damp interior now. Animals had died in there. Hard to imagine even a homeless person sheltering here, even in summer. But Amelie had said nobody went inside much. Just lingered here out of the rain. Brief shelter. Still.

He remembered Amelie telling him about a TV show she'd seen, about dream interpretation. If you dream about a house or a building, Amelie said, you're really dreaming about yourself—your mind. "And the attic or the basement is sort of your unconscious self. Maybe you don't like what you find there, or maybe it's something great you forgot about. But either way, it's part of you. It's your secret self." Maybe, he thought, I dreamed this building. It would be appropriate. Down into his jerrybuilt and crumbling soul, echoes of his own voice rumbling through these ruined corridors.

Moving into the darkness, he thumbed the switch on his flashlight. The beam lanced out ahead.

Soon he was aware of another human presence—of the distant, stealthy tread of feet, faint echoes at the threshold of perception: a whisper in this frigid air, but revealing. He didn't doubt that the presence was Roch. Too many signs had pointed this way; the truth was too obvious. He tried to track the distant footfalls as he moved, to range on them . . . this was his uniqueness after all, his secret weapon. . . .

But he was sidetracked by his thoughts. It was as if the sound of his own thinking had grown intolerably loud, a din that drowned out the external world. He recognized this as akin to the feverishness that had overtaken him last night, or maybe the same feverishness, a dementia that had never entirely retreated. He was dying, after all. Or, if not dying, then retreating into some utterly new form, a dim shape just emerging from the darkness. Which was, when you came right down to it, a kind of dying.

He stumbled against a damp concrete wall. Vertigo. This wouldn't do at all. He had entered the world of Greek and Latin nouns: vertigo, dementia, kinaesthesia, aphasia. . . . *Too soon,* he thought.

He thought about Roch.

There was a skittering from a dark room beyond the reach of his flashlight beam. Not Roch: some animal, maybe a rat; he hurried past.

He remembered Roch from their confrontation in Amelie's apartment. A big man, muscular, no real threat—not then—but John recalled also his deeper sense of the man as a fierce kettle of hostility, at explosive pressure. But "hostility," what an inadequate word! It was an anger as purified and symmetrical as a laser beam, far more potent than any physical threat and more difficult to overcome. John was, at this moment, more than a little frightened of it.

He had counted on his old abilities here, the superhuman edge, but since last night that surety had blurred. The edges of things ran together, events happened too quickly, some internal clock had slowed down. His impression of the corridor now, in the sway of his flashlight beam over concrete and blackened ceiling beams, was more vivid than it ought to be but less informative: he was hard-pressed to extract the implications of a footprint or an echo. Where was Roch? Where was Amelie?

Moving deeper now, he discovered a wooden ladder leading up through a gap in the ceiling where a staircase might once have been. The rungs of the ladder were not dusty but seemed almost polished, and this, at least, he could interpret. He switched off the flashlight and in the darkness detected a fainter light flickering above him. It wasn't much, but it was something to follow.

At the top of the ladder he groped his way onto a horizontal surface and flicked the flashlight back on. He was in a narrower, older corridor; the wallboard had been pried away in places and the yellow lathing peeked through. The flashlight beam paled away in an atmosphere of dust motes. He moved still deeper, approaching the heart of the building.

He was totally enclosed now—the thought inspired a new, nauseating wave of vertigo. He heard faint sounds lost in their own echoes, which might be voices, or water dripping down these old posts and columns, or the sound of whimpering. His own footsteps seemed impossibly loud, and the dust was choking.

Then, without warning, he turned a corner into a long windowless room which was *not* empty. First he saw the flickering Sterno fire, then Amelie bound at the wrists and ankles and squirming against the floor. She was wearing grimy jeans and a striped top, a soiled ski jacket; her eyes were vague but she looked at him pleadingly.

"Amelie." He was hardly aware of saying it. Maybe it was Benjamin who spoke. Benjamin's memories were powerfully present as he stooped to untie her. Their conversations, meals together, arguments, their lovemaking. She was tied with nylon clothesline and his fingers were too numb to manage the knots; but he had a Swiss Army knife in his pocket and he pulled it out and fumbled open the blade. Amelie watched curiously, as if she couldn't quite decide who he was; which was reasonable, after all, because he wasn't entirely certain himself . . . he had lost track of his own name. Words were suddenly elusive; he imagined them (the vision was crystalline in his mind) as a flock of birds startled into a cold blue sky.

The blade parted the cords. Her hands, faintly blue, sprang apart. But maybe Amelie had lost her words, too. She was pointing and gasping, backing away. . . .

Too late, John understood her wild gesturing. He turned in time to see Roch rush forward from the doorway. Roch had a length of pipe in his right hand and John focused briefly on it, on the islands of verdigris laced across the copper, green in the flickering firelight. In its own way it was beautiful. Mesmerizing.

Roch smiled.

"Get out of here," John told Amelie.

Roch brought the pipe down. John managed to catch the first

blow against the open palm of his left hand, but the shock traveled up his arm to the shoulder and seemed to unhinge something there. The arm fell limp as Amelie scurried past. Passing, she slipped and kicked the burning Sterno across the floor. It spilled against an exposed spruce stud; the light was briefly dim and then flared much brighter . . . but John's attention was on Roch, who had reared back for a second blow. John tried to veer away, but something was wrong here: the weapon came down too fast, or his legs were unsteady—*everything* happened too fast—and he was aware of the miscalculation but helpless to correct it as Roch brought the pipe down in a clean trajectory that intersected precisely with John's skull; the impact was explosive. He felt as if he were flying away in every direction at once—and then there was only the darkness.

28

The blow connected solidly.

Roch allowed himself a brief rush of satisfaction, then turned and ran after Amelie.

Running, he transferred the pipe to a loop in his belt and took the flashlight in his right hand. He trained the beam on her; but she was already a surprising distance down the corridor . . . he must have been too cautious with the narcotics, must have let the time get away from him.

He tripped over a spur of concrete and almost dropped the flashlight; he managed to recover, but it gained Amelie some critical time. He stabbed the flashlight forward and saw her disappear down the empty stairwell—a miracle she had found the ladder in this darkness, but of course it was his own light, his own trusty Eveready, that had led her there. "Bitch!" he screamed, and drew out the copper pipe and bounced it against an aluminum conduit suspended from the ceiling. The sound rang out around him like a bell, metallic and cacophonous in this closed space. Amelie ducked her head down below the floor . . . but Roch didn't follow.

He was frozen in place . . . paralyzed by the sudden and terrible suspicion that he had done something momentous, something irrevocable . . . that he had jackknifed off the high board into an empty pool. How had he arrived in this dark, cavernous hallway? Basically, what the fuck was he *doing* here?

But there was no answer, only the keening of the ventilator shafts down these blind, scabbed walls.

He clenched his teeth and suppressed the doubt. Maybe there was some truth to it, maybe he *had* taken the dive without looking; but when you get this far, he thought, it just doesn't matter anymore. You're up there in the spotlight and you tuck and spin because it's the focal point of your entire life even if you don't understand it, you just *know*, so *fuck* all that pain and death that's rushing up at you; that's *after*. Now is *now*.

He hefted the copper pipe and turned back to the burning room.

29

Susan saw Amelie stumble away from the shadow of the building and knew at once that something had gone terribly wrong.

Amelie was sick or hurt. She took five lunging steps into the snow and then seemed to lose momentum—stopped, wobbled, and fell forward.

Susan ran out from the cover of the trees. The snow hindered every step; it was like running in a nightmare. She looked up briefly as she passed into the shadow of the warehouse. The building seemed to generate its own chill, potent even in the still winter air.

She put her arms around Amelie and lifted her up. Amelie was trembling. She was cold to the touch, and her eyes wandered aimlessly. . . . Susan guessed some kind of drug might be involved.

"Amelie!" Some recognition flickered in her eyes. "Amelie, is John inside? Is he all right?"

"He's in there," Amelie managed.

"Is he hurt?"

"He's with Roch."

Susan stifled a powerful urge to go in after him.

She took a deep breath. *Do what you have to.* "I'll take you to the car," she said. "Then we can call the police."

———

They crossed the railroad tracks and ducked under the link fence toward the Honda, both of them breathless and gasping by the time they reached the car. Amelie doubled over against the lid of the trunk, her cheek pressed to the cold metal. Susan turned back toward the warehouse, one edge of it still visible over a stand of snowy pine trees. She shielded her eyes and frowned at what she saw: a thick plume of white smoke had begun to waft upward from the western corner of the building.

30

The warehouse had been stripped bare years ago. Everything even remotely valuable had been sold or stolen. There was no furniture left to burn; the floor was pressed concrete; the exterior walls were brick. But there were ancient kiln-dried spruce studs; there were pressboard dividing walls where these lofty spaces had been partitioned into offices; there was an immense volume of sub-code insulation that had been installed by the contractor as a cost-cutting measure during a 1965 renovation. Altogether, there was plenty to burn.

John awoke to the burning.

—————

The Sterno can had spilled flaming jelly across the floor, the bulk of it next to three exposed wooden structural studs.

The wood was porous and spectacularly dry. The flames licked at it, paused as if to gather strength, then ran upward to the ceiling beams and through an open airway to the third floor, where they encountered a five-foot-high stack of the Saturday edition of the Toronto *Sun* dated 1979 through 1981.

The flames relished it.

Awake now—dimly—John rolled away from the heat. A glowing ember flaked down from the ceiling and scorched the skin of his wrist. His lungs felt raw, sandpapered. He opened his eyes.

He saw the flames running across the ceiling in freshets, like water. Where the room had been dark, it was now bright with a sinister light. He lifted a hand to shade his vision.

His head hurt. When he moved, the pain was dizzying; nausea constricted his throat. The agony was so generalized as to seem sourceless; then he touched his head above his left ear and felt the pulpy texture of the skin there. The hair was matted and wet. His hand, when he pulled it away, glistened in the firelight. This wetness was blood.

Blood and fire all around him.

He remembered Roch.

––––––––

The overheated air created by the flames was vastly lighter than the cold, stagnant air surrounding it. It shot upward almost volcanically, coursing through the abandoned building like a river cut loose from the restraints of gravity. Where stairways had fallen, it rose through the gaping spaces. It discovered flues and airways. It was merely warm by the time it reached the top of the building, but still hot enough to seek out an icy five-foot gap where the ceiling had collapsed and to rise, lazily at first, into the still afternoon air.

This was how Susan saw it from the Honda: a waft of almost pure white smoke.

It gathered strength.

––––––––

John understood that something was broken inside him. That was the way it felt, and it might be literally true; Roch had hit him pretty hard. He was confused about this place and he was confused about whether he was "John" or "Benjamin"—or what these names implied—and just about the only thing he was *not* confused about was the urgency of getting out of the building. The building was on fire; it was burning; he could be trapped here. That much was clear.

He managed to stand up.

He saw the flashlight on the floor and picked it up. He could see well enough in the firelight but he might need this later. There was a thin veil of acrid smoke all around him—fortunately, most of it was still being drawn up by the rising heat. That might change, however. And even this faint haze was choking. Combustion products. Toxic gases. These words floated up from memory, briefly vivid in his mind: he could read them, like printed words on paper, in the space behind his eyelids. But the danger was real and imminent.

He staggered into the hallway, where Roch was waiting for him.

––––––––

Roch came forward in a lunge with the copper pipe extended, grinning hugely. John knew that Roch meant to kill him and leave him here where the fire would consume his body. He understood this by the expression on Roch's face. There was nothing mysterious about it. Blunt, burning hatred. Once again he watched the slow ballistic swing of the pipe above Roch's head and the arc it would follow downward: this was familiar, too.

The ballet of his own death.

But not yet, John decided.

It was not even a thought. It was a denial so absolute that it felt like a seizure. He took a step back, hefted the big hardware-store flashlight and threw it at Roch. The flashlight whirled as it flew, end over end, and it seemed to John that Roch was staring at it, perplexed and wholly attentive, as it impacted squarely against his forehead.

Roch teetered on his heels, lunging forward with the pipe-section for ballast. No good. He sat down hard on the concrete floor. A line of blood seeped out from the impact point on his forehead.

He looked at John with mute, angry amazement.

"Son of a bitch!" he managed.

Began climbing to his feet again, pipe in hand.

John turned and ran.

But *who* had thrown the flashlight?

This question occupied a brightly lit corner of his mind as he staggered down the increasingly dark and smoky corridor.

Because, he *felt different.*

Not John or Benjamin.

Some third thing.

It rose and shifted inside him even now. It was large and still wordless. It didn't have a name; it had never had a name. Some new presence. Or maybe not: not new at all.

Maybe, John thought, it had been there all along.

Roch had cut him off from the ladder where he had climbed up to the second floor; John ran in the opposite direction.

The fire was large and potent now, able to leapfrog the stony breaks between oases of wood and insulation. No part of the building was safe. Already, on the floor above, two of the tiny wire-reinforced windows had been blown out of their frames by the pressure of the burning. Flame jetted from the empty spaces, a newly crowned infant king surveying his kingdom.

The fire created its own weather. Throughout the eastern half of the structure, air that had lain stagnant for years began to stir. Locked or boarded doors groaned against their restraints. Shuttered windows rattled. The sour dust of limestone and decayed animal droppings stirred and lifted. The fire drew in gusts of clean air from the winter afternoon, and for one paradoxical moment it seemed as if a kind of spring had come.

John felt the air on his face, a good sign. It meant he was moving away from the main body of the fire. He had decided there must be another way down; it was only a question of finding it. But the light had dimmed to a smoky nimbus; he had lost the flashlight and soon he would be groping on his hands and knees. And Roch was close behind him. He heard the footsteps, though he could no longer calculate direction and distance.

He understood, too, that the fire had grown large enough that it might encircle him. That if it did, he would be helpless.

Strange, he thought, to die without knowing his own name.

———

The darkness now was absolute, interrupted in rare moments by the flicker of Roch's flashlight from behind. John toiled onward as quickly as he dared. But the air was warm and choking. He didn't have much margin anymore, and he knew it.

When he saw a glimmer of light down the corridor he was afraid that it might be the fire circling around from the front. He slowed to a walk, groped ahead cautiously, then stood for a moment surrounded by this dim aurora before it registered as window-light.

The windows were tiny glass rectangles set in a wickerwork of framing. They rose from waist level to the ceiling, and they were so thickly crusted with grime that he hadn't recognized them at first for what they were.

He pushed against one of the panes with both hands, but it didn't yield. This was carpentry as old as the building itself, Victorian and hugely solid. He took away his hands and carried enough dirt with them that the prints let through a brighter beam of light, hand-shaped in the smoky air.

He looked around. He wanted a brick, a pipe like Roch's, anything . . . but the corridor was bare.

Roch's flashlight flickered behind him.

Sighing, John pulled off his jacket and wrapped it around his right hand. Bracing himself, he drove his fist directly into the thick glass.

It was like punching rock—bruising, even through the cloth. But the glass splintered and fell away, leaving a razor-toothed space where cool air came flooding in.

The panes of glass were maybe twelve inches square, and he knocked out ten of them so rapidly that there was no time to notice the shards that ripped through the lining of the jacket and pierced his hand and wrist. The pain was momentary and irrelevant. When the glass was gone, he kicked and ripped at the wooden latticework until there was a hole big enough to fit through.

He heard Roch almost directly behind him now, but there was time to ascertain that he himself was directly above the old loading bay; that there was a roof below him, two-by-fours covered with lathing and tarry shingles, some of this eroded by the weather . . . not exactly a firm footing; time enough, too, to see that the fire had reached the west end of the loading-bay roof and was spreading wildly.

He turned his head and saw Roch running down the corridor toward him, his features clenched in a concentration so total that John was reminded of a master chess-player—the same all-consuming focus. The copper pipe-length was cocked at an angle, ready. John leaped forward and down onto the canted roof of the loading bay and then spread-eagled himself against it. The shingles were already warm where his cheek pressed against them. Something was burning down below. But the air was clean.

He began inching downward. With luck, he might make it to the edge before the flames caught up with him. Then he could swing down to ground level. If there *wasn't* time—he could let himself roll and tumble, take his chances on what might be down below.

———

In the distance—already audible, though it escaped John's aware-ness—the firetrucks howled their sirens.

The smoke that had drifted up lazily only minutes before was darker, and it boiled skyward in massive gouts. The roof of the building had drifted over with snow, but that was melting—a sudden waterfall developed where the roof sagged toward the southeast corner—while the snow nearest the flames was simply vaporized by the heat. The hissing was as loud as the crackle of the fire; Susan, running back down the tracks from the pay-phone and the Honda, was startled by the sound.

———

The makeshift roof over the loading bay was just twelve feet above the ground at the lowest point of its slope. What John had con-templated doing might have been safe: to let himself tumble down and hope the snow would cushion his fall. But he was trans-fixed by the sight of Roch stepping up into the frame of the broken window, a mist of smoke writhing after him; clinging to the frame to keep himself from falling, shards of glass piercing his hands as John's hands had been pierced, the copper pipe fallen and rolling away—missing John's head by three or four inches—over the roof and out of sight.

Hanging there, Roch looked down at John in a blaze of distilled hatred—and then across at the western edge of the roof, where the flames had begun to creep forward.

He braced his feet and took his hands off the window frame.

The roof was old and weathered. It had been designed to carry a calculated weight of snow—barely. In the years since it was erected, dry rot had invaded the studs; ice and water had pried up the shingles and rusted the nails. It could not support more than a fraction of its calculated load.

In particular, it couldn't support Roch.

His left foot pierced the shingles first. Roch's eyes widened as he slipped to thigh-level, like a man in quicksand, his right leg buckling under him and the shingles peeling away with sharp, successive snaps. His right knee penetrated similarly, and then he seemed to hesitate for a moment, straddling a joist, hands clawing at open air . . . and then the joist separated with a sound like a gunshot and Roch simply disappeared.

There was a sickening moment of absolute silence, then the thud as Roch impacted against the loading-bay platform below.

———

John raised his head.

He could see Susan running toward the building, Amelie not far behind her. Those two were safe. That was good.

He could have joined them. He knew what to do. Let go, tuck and roll, let his momentum carry him away from the loading dock and hope that the snowdrift would break his fall. He was aware of the beat of his heart and the onrushing eagerness of the flames—how could he do anything else?

But he felt himself inching forward, up the angle of the roof toward the hole Roch had made.

He braced his fingers against the shingles at the edge and looked down.

Roch was lying motionless, his hips at an unnatural angle and his eyes closed, the flames advancing from the western end of the loading bay and already hot enough to singe his eyebrows.

One more experiment, John thought.

Just one.

———

But maybe it wasn't an experiment. Maybe it was something more important.

He felt himself straddling a cross-joist and wrapping his arms around it, then levering himself out over this high vacant space, swinging down toward Roch and the burning platform, and he understood with a sudden piercing clarity that he wasn't John or Benjamin anymore. Some new being had grown into the vacuum of his skin, nurtured by his fever and the sudden desert heat of the flames—a fragment of self so fundamental that it had lurked undiscovered beneath all the latticework of words. It had existed even before he learned the word *I;* an *uninvented* self.

He let go of the creaking joist and dropped in a crouch next to Roch, feeling a sudden pain in his ankles and knees and spine but still able to stand.

His vision blurred in the smoke. He was aware of the blood on his hands, the cuts circling his wrists, the throbbing in his temple where Roch had struck him with the pipe. He was not sure he had the strength for this.

For this *experiment.*

He kneeled against the hot floorboards and slipped his arm around Roch.

Roch was not wholly unconscious. His eyelids flickered open as John lifted him up. Briefly, he struggled; but his legs dangled limp and useless and the pain of his injuries must have been excruciating—his eyes riveted shut again.

The flames closed in from the western edge of the loading bay and began to lick out from the warehouse doors. John glanced up and it was like staring into a furnace; his skin prickled and itched. Overhead, the joists were popping their nails with a sound like gunfire. Embers rained down all around him.

He should leave this burden and simply run—

But the thought was evanescent; it vanished into the tindery air.

Roch's legs would not support him; it was like hefting a two-hundred-pound sack of sand. Roch opened his eyes once more as John hauled him up. He did not struggle; seemed only to watch, almost impassively . . . his eyes were fixed on John's eyes and his face, now, was only inches away. His eyes seemed to radiate the single blunt message: "I'm not one of you!"—and John understood, in a final flash of inhuman insight, that Roch had willfully set himself apart; that when he looked at other human beings he saw protoplasm, bags of flesh, vessels that might contain the elements of hatred or contempt . . . but never anything of Roch.

Roch was only Roch, the only one of his kind, alone in his uniqueness. And across that vast escarpment there was no bridge or road or trail: the divide was as absolute as a vacuum. And John perceived that this was not some flaw of character or nurture; it was more profound, a trick of gestation, a stitch in the glial network . . . somehow, it was *built in.* . . . My God, John thought, he's not even altogether human. . . .

He pinned Roch's arms in his own and dragged him toward the snow. Roch was stunningly heavy, a dead weight. But the fire was close enough to raise smoke from their clothes and John drew some strength from that. He pulled Roch along with his heels dragging against the steaming floorboards. He felt Roch's breath against his neck. Roch opened his eyes again, now two blank wells of unimaginable hostility—and maybe something else.

Maybe a question.

"Because I don't want to be what you are," John said. The words came out punctuated by his gasping, overwhelmed by the roar of the flames; but patient, gentle. "Because I'm *tired* of that."

———

He carried Roch away from the burning platform of the loading bay, into the steaming snow and beyond into the thick snow that had not yet melted and where the reflection of the fire was gaudy and strange.

In the end, he was only dimly aware of Amelie as she pried at his fingers. His embrace of Roch was fierce and hysterical. But he gave it up at last.

PART IV
RESULTS

31

Spring is the rainy season in Los Angeles, but today the air was cool and clean; the sky was blue; the smog had rolled away in a vast tide of Pacific air. Susan placed a wreath of flowers on her father's grave and stood up, smoothing her dress. The sun picked out a fleck of mica on the headstone, like the winking of an eye.

Daddy, she thought, *what do I do now?*

She meant: about John.

For seven weeks after the warehouse fire John had been comatose in a Toronto hospital. Susan had visited him daily; she had helped to nurse him. It hurt to see him silent and still in his hospital bed, contained in a sleep so absolute that it was a flicker away from death. Sleep like another country, Susan thought; some place where he had retreated, miles and miles and miles away.

But it was not his sleep that had sent her fleeing to California. It was his waking up. "John is awake," Dr. Kyriakides had said, and the announcement touched off in her a fierce, visceral panic.

It was impossible to face the prospect of pushing through the door of his hospital room and finding him changed beyond recognition.

So she bought a ticket for the next available flight and stayed with her mother. She kept some secrets, told some lies, moped around in the fenced backyard while the ultraviolet burned her body brown. But there was no avoiding this ritual journey to the cemetery.

Daddy, what now?

Silent earth.

She looked up. A silver dot was traversing the blue sky, probably an airliner out of L.A. International. But Susan didn't want to think about airliners, which suggested travel, which suggested that this sunny interlude was not any kind of solution . . . that pretty soon she ought to buy a return ticket, get herself on one of those planes—

—cross that border—

Startled, she looked back at the grave.

It was her father's voice. Her own thought, of course; but it was unmistakably his resonant, deep, and familiar voice. Drawn up, she thought, not from the grave but from the well of memory. Maybe this is why we invent people, Susan thought: because we cannot bear the loss of them.

She touched the mica-flecked granite headstone.

Daddy? Should I go back there? Is that what I should do?

But the answer was obvious.

That would be the wise thing, Susan.

Funny way to hold a conversation. But then, she thought, it's always hard, when the silence has been so long and so awkward.

32

Amelie decided to visit Roch in the hospital: just once, because she had to.

It was safe; she was safe from him there. Anyway, she thought, the whole world is pretty much safe from Roch, now and forever.

He looked up sullenly from the bed. Roch had lost a lot of weight; his singed hair had been cropped short. He looked like a convict, Amelie thought . . . which she guessed he was, or at least potentially. She hadn't pressed charges, but the holding company that owned the warehouse was pretty pissed off. (Even though their insurance must have paid them off in full—the fire must have been like hitting a Vegas jackpot, considering the condition of the property.)

But Roch didn't care. He just looked up at her with his hollow eyes. And Amelie felt perversely guilty for coming here at all . . . she was still that vulnerable to his anger.

"I'm going away," she said.

He didn't answer. Silence was one of the few weapons he had left.

She went on, "I know this is a shitty time and all, considering what happened, but I don't think I owe you anything anymore. I guess that's pretty obvious. I mean, it's too bad what happened, but it isn't my fault."

"I almost killed you," he said. The words were slurred with medication, but totally sincere. She felt his anger simmering inside him. He had been insulted in a way he could barely comprehend. The *last* insult, Amelie thought, if only he would let it be. "I should have," he added.

Well, maybe she had made a mistake, coming here. But it was important, not just for Roch's sake but for Amelie's: important to talk to his doctors . . . important to *see* him; important to prove to herself that she need never be afraid of him again. The doctors called it "a spinal cord injury sustained during his fall," but Amelie knew it was really more than that. It was her protection. It was a guarantee that Roch would never be able to hurt her again.

Still—she felt sorry for him, lying broken in this hospital bed.

It should not have been possible, this surge of pity.

Mysterious.

She had talked to John about Roch, not long before all this happened. John had encountered Roch only that one time, in her apartment, but John had guessed a few things about him. He asked, "Was your mother an alcoholic?" and Amelie said, "Well—you could say that. She drank pretty heavy sometimes."

"Before Roch was born? When she was pregnant?"

"Probably. I think so. Why?"

He told her, "There's a condition called 'fetal alcohol syndrome.' Sometimes it causes retardation. Sometimes it has other effects, more subtle."

"You think Roch has that?"

"It's possible. All that unfocused anger. The alcohol interferes with fetal development, particularly the development of the brain. It has a sort of scattering effect on the neurons. The glial cells—"

Amelie waved her hand. "Maybe Roch has that. I don't know. Does it matter? Lots of people have lots of problems. When it comes down to it, what matters is what you *do*—right? Not what you *are.*"

And John had smiled a strange, distant smile and nodded his head slowly. "Yes, Amelie. That's what matters."

She told Roch goodbye now, and left the room.

———

Amelie had stayed on at the big house north of the city. Kyriakides had said it was okay. But enough, she thought, was enough. John was back from the hospital now. And Benjamin—

Benjamin was dead.

Well, maybe that wasn't exactly true. John wasn't Benjamin anymore; but he wasn't exactly John, either. Privately, Amelie figured he was something that John and Benjamin had both needed to become. Maybe something they had been all along. Something more basic, more raw, more true.

Maybe what she had loved about Benjamin was this *becoming.* Benjamin had been half finished and wholly innocent. Benjamin was a coming-to-life, an *event.* And that was finished. And so her part of it was finished.

Almost finished.

She packed two Tourister suitcases. She could come back for her other stuff later, when she found a place. Her little Sanyo stereo . . . Kyriakides could keep it, or Susan, or John. She didn't care.

On her way out, she stopped off at the big study where Dr. Kyriakides was scribbling away in some kind of notebook, his glasses practically toppling off the end of his nose. She stood in the doorway until he noticed her.

He spotted the suitcases. "You're leaving?"

She nodded.

"Do you have a place to go?"

"I can rent a room until I find an apartment. Maybe I can get my old job back."

"I want you to know—you're free to room here as long as you like."

"I think it would be better to get away."

Kyriakides frowned. . . . *Something he wants to say,* Amelie thought . . . then he cleared his throat.

She waited.

He said, "Amelie . . . I know about the pregnancy."

"Christ!" She was appalled. "Who told you that? It was Collingwood, right? The clinic doctor told Collingwood and Collingwood told you. Jesus! So much for fucking privacy!"

"This is an unusual situation," Kyriakides said. "I assume it's John's child?"

Amelie considered walking out. She didn't owe Kyriakides anything. He hadn't earned this conversation.

Some impulse restrained her. *"Benjamin's* child," she said. An important distinction. "You bet it is."

"Calm down. I didn't engineer this invasion of your privacy for the sake of voyeurism. The point is, I want to help."

"Help?"

"Help the child. I can arrange for money, a place for you to stay—"

"I don't want to be a fucking research project!"

"I don't want you to be. It's just that I feel like a grandfather to this child. I've thought about it a lot. About the past, the present. I think now I might not have given John everything he deserved. I would like a chance to do better. Even in a small way. This is—" He spread his hands on the desk. "This is important to me."

He means it, Amelie thought. The offer was absolutely sincere. She couldn't say exactly why it bothered her so much. Still— "I appreciate it," she said. "But we'll be fine."

"You can't be sure of that."

"I'm not totally alone. I have friends. If I need help, I'll get in touch." With John, she thought privately, or whatever John was now. He had earned that connection. Kyriakides had not.

"You don't understand what I'm offering."

The tone was imperious. She frowned. "Maybe I don't."

"You wouldn't have to work. No more tawdry little restaurant jobs. No more cold-water apartments. All that would be over. And there's nothing I want in exchange. No deal to make. Nothing to give up. Just say yes."

She picked up her luggage. "Thank you anyway."

She turned to leave.

His voice boomed after her: "What can you give to that child? You have nothing! My God! One more slutty welfare mother with one more worthless infant—is *that* what you want to be?"

"I'm not good enough for you?" She turned to face him. "You want me to be something better. You want this baby to be something better. But you don't even know what that word means. You talk about people like they're bugs, insects. You say you hate them because they're cruel and stupid, but *you* can take a life and twist it all out of shape—how are you different?"

"I've seen more cruelty than you have. Cruelty and destructive stupidity. God help us, is it wrong to want to change that?"

They were talking about John now, Amelie realized, not the baby. "Susan told me what happened with Marga. You used her and you bought her off. She was a lump of clay, right? A tool. 'One more slutty welfare mother.' But you can't make a better human being out of that—that *hate*. I just don't think you can."

His face was brick red. "Obviously you don't understand anything."

"I do," Amelie said. "I understand that's what you wanted John to be. A better human being. But that's not what happened. Not better. A *broken* human being."

It struck home. Kyriakides sat down heavily. For a moment he seemed to struggle for breath.

"I know," he said at last. "You're right. That's what he is now —broken."

"No," Amelie said. "That's what he was *before.*" She picked up her bags. "Now, he's *better.*"

———

She waited for a southbound bus at the foot of the driveway. The snow had mostly gone and the crocuses were coming up. It was a cold day but bright; there was a little breeze blowing. Kind of nice, Amelie thought. Not a bad day at all.

A bus pulled up to the curb, sighing diesel fumes. She climbed inside, paid her fare, stowed her Touristers under the seat. The bus eased away and began to pick up speed.

She resisted the urge to look back. Time to look ahead, she thought. A clean horizon and this ribbon of road. Her future was up there somewhere, waiting to be invented; her baby was waiting to be born.

A new life, she thought, but not starting over as if the past had never happened. She would carry it with her: *all* the memories. Not just Benjamin but Roch, too. *These things are what I am.* It was possible to make a better life—for herself, for this baby—but not out of shame. Not out of hating what had happened. *You can't do that:* she had told Kyriakides so, and she believed it.

New life inside her. Anything was possible.

You'll be my baby, she thought. *Amelie's baby. And that's not such a terrible thing to be.*

She smiled to herself, settled back into the seat, turned to the window. Outside, everywhere along the broad margin of the road, the snow was melting in the sun.

33

Susan called from California when her ticket was confirmed.

"He's not John," Dr. Kyriakides told her. "Be prepared for that. But he's not Benjamin, either. He's awake and functional and I'm certain he'll eventually be able to hold a job, to lead a normal life. But he isn't the person we knew."

He isn't the person you *created*, Susan thought. And she wondered if that wasn't John's ultimate act of revenge, a score that had finally been evened.

She said, "I'm prepared."

"His memory is erratic, but I think he'll know you."

"That's good," Susan said.

———

She took a cab from Pearson Airport. Dr. Kyriakides met her at the door of the house.

Such an ordinary house, Susan thought.

"I told him you were coming. He's looking forward to it."

"Thank you," Susan said, and moved toward the stairs.

"One more thing," Kyriakides said. "John was cleaning up his desk today. He found this. He asked me to give it to you."

It was a five-inch Dysan floppy disk in a paper sleeve. It had her name written on it—"FOR SUSAN" in block capitals.

"It's from before," Kyriakides said.

———

She knocked gently on the door of his room and pushed inside.

John was asleep.

He had pulled a chair up to the window—watching the spring clouds, Susan guessed—and he had fallen asleep there. She moved to touch him on the shoulder, then remembered the disk in her hand.

Maybe she shouldn't wake him.

She sat down at his computer and slid the disk into its slot.

It began to run when she turned on the machine. The disk drive whined; a hard disk answered in deeper tones. It was not an ordinary PC; John had done something to the microprocessors. Susan wondered if she would be able to work it. But the monitor blinked to life all by itself.

It displayed, first of all, a date: the material was several years old. This would be, Susan calculated, when John was living on his island, before she met him, before the return of Benjamin: something from John's deep immersion in cellular biology.

The date disappeared and there was more whining from the drives as a plodding animation appeared on the screen. Susan blinked at it, surprised. It was a metastatic tumor cell—it looked like diagrams she had seen of the 3LL mouse carcinoma, a common experimental lab tumor. The perspective closed in suddenly on the cell surface, where John had ideographed certain molecules: she recognized collagenase and the MHC glycoproteins. These dissolved in turn into ball-and-stick perspective drawings of their molecular structure. A new molecule appeared at the right side of the screen, one that Susan did not recognize, although John had labeled it meticulously—a novel protein, synthetic or even hypothetical. Suddenly it closed on the MHC glycoprotein and bound with it in a violent flurry of activity. The product was a fragmented chain.

Susan realized she was holding her breath.

The screen blanked, then refreshed with the original metastatic cell . . . exploded and dead.

It was a magic bullet. A designer molecule: the screen filled with a protocol for its synthesis.

Not a cure for cancer, Susan thought, but at least a cure for its metastasis, a way to interrupt the fearsome colonization of a human body by tumor cells. As a postoperative therapy it could prolong lives indefinitely. She thought of her father, rendered mute, and then dying, murdered by his metastasis before he could recover the courage for words.

She remembered, too, what John had told her on that cold January day before he walked into the warehouse and out of the world: *There are lives I could have saved . . . thousands, maybe even hundreds of thousands.*

This was what he meant. He had devised this program for his own satisfaction, an "experiment." If he had made it public or even submitted it anonymously to some journal or some laboratory —it might be in production already, Susan thought, or at least well down the FDA pipeline.

She withdrew the floppy disk—carefully!—and looked at the label again.

For Susan.

She faced the bed. He opened his eyes.

———

There was so much he didn't remember.

Waking up, seeing the woman, he was acutely aware of his handicap. He had lost a great deal over the duration of his fever: memory, vocabulary, time. The loss was endurable mainly because it was so far-reaching—impossible to mourn the absence of a thing he could only vaguely recall. But there were times, like this, when the immensity of his loss was painful and obvious.

Her face was familiar.

I know that face. Memories surfaced and then winked away, elusive as fish in a still, deep pool. He remembered her face next to his, her eyes on his eyes, snow on a window, words spoken softly in a silence that had seemed as large as the night; her name—

"Susan," he said.

She smiled tentatively. Once he had been able to read the nuances of her face as simply as he might read a book. He remembered the odd sense that she was transparent, skin and skull invisible, the trace of her thoughts etched there as clearly as animal tracks in fresh snow. But now there was only her face, opaque but pretty; her eyes only eyes, very blue.

Another fragment of memory flashed past. He said, "You saved my life."

"No," she said hurriedly. "No, not really."

"You did," he affirmed.

He sat up cross-legged across the bed and regarded her seriously. "Did you talk to Dr. Kyriakides?"

She nodded.

"Then you know what I am. I'm not Benjamin. But I'm not John, either. They're gone. Both gone."

"You've changed," she said. "Well, I've changed too. That's not so strange."

"You loved John," he said.

Susan blushed, opened her mouth and then closed it.

"Yes," she said finally. "I loved him, and it's hard saying it that way—as if he's dead. But I don't think that's really true. I think there was something in him he never talked about or acknowledged—maybe it was in Benjamin, too—something that doesn't go away because it's too basic, it's built into every cell. I know that's not scientific but I believe it."

He regarded her with open, surprised interest.

"I'm talking too much. But I want you to know why I came. I didn't come expecting John—not the old John. I came to see you." She hesitated. "I guess I wanted to say, well, here I am if you need me and I have a car parked outside if you ever need to get away." Her fists were clenched and she was avoiding his eyes. "I couldn't *not* come." But she looked at him, finally. "I came because if you need to talk to someone you shouldn't keep silent —because it'll kill you, doing that."

She looked at him across the room, her eyes full of doubt— surprised at what she'd said, he guessed; worried at what he might think.

He smiled.

"Those are good reasons," he said.

————

They talked, and he discovered that certain memories were not so elusive after all; that the sound of her voice or the choice of a word evoked echoes from his life before the fire. Maybe this was how "normal" memory worked—the past made subtle and mysterious, forgotten moments welling up miraculously whole at the touch of a hand or the turning of a head.

"We used to play chess," he said. "I remember."

"That's right. We can play again, if you like."

"I'm not sure—I don't know if I can."

"It'll come back to you," she said. "I can help. We can learn from each other."

That's true, he thought, and memory came welling up once again: of her voice, simple words, the shape of her ear in a darkened room—*Of course we can learn from each other.*

It wouldn't be the first time.

DATE DUE

PUBLIC LIBRARY
Stoneham, MA

S

Wilson, Robert C.
The divide